SCARY STORIES FOR STORMY NIGHTS #6

Allen B. Ury

LOWELL HOUSE JUVENILE

LOS ANGELES

CONTEMPORARY BOOKS

CHICAGO

Library of Congress Catalog Card Number: 97-075406
ISBN: 1-56565-901-5

Publisher: Jack Artenstein
Editor in Chief, Roxbury Park Books: Michael Artenstein
Director of Publishing Services: Rena Copperman
Managing Editor: Lindsey Hay

Lowell House books can be purchased at special discounts when ordered in bulk for premiums and special sales.
Contact Department TC at the following address:

Lowell House
2020 Avenue of the Stars, Suite 300
Los Angeles, CA 90067

Manufactured in the United States of America
10 9 8 7 6 5 4 3 2 1

CONTENTS

※ ※ ※

BEDTIME STORIES

I'D NEVER BEEN AWAY FROM HOME UNTIL THAT summer I went to Camp Waupaca. And I've never been as scared.

It's tough enough for a 12-year-old boy to spend a whole month up in Wisconsin's north woods with a bunch of strange kids, deprived of television, video games, fast food, shopping malls, and the rest of life's necessities. And the counselors didn't make the experience any easier. Especially Brad Hollman.

Brad was a tall, blond, 19-year-old college student from Fond du Lac who claimed to be majoring in physical education. But I think his real major was torturing kids. Not that he practiced the kind of cruelty some counselors did. He never forced us to do a hundred push-ups in the pouring rain or to eat raw liver or anything like that. No, Brad's favorite brand of meanness was far more wicked. His torture was *psychological*. And it usually took the form of bedtime horror stories.

Yeah, Brad was the Stephen King of the campfire. Every night he'd take the 15 of us out to the barbecue pit, get a good log fire going, and then scare us spitless with his intricate, vivid tales of murder and mayhem. He'd tell ghost stories, monster stories, stories about rampaging aliens and frozen cavepeople brought back to life. But his favorite stories were about escaped lunatics. I mean, he just *loved* to tell tales about homicidal maniacs who had busted out of insane asylums and were rampaging through the countryside, ambushing teenagers parked on Lovers' Lane, terrorizing hapless baby-sitters, and leaving severed heads, bloody arms, plucked eyeballs, and other disgusting calling cards in their wakes.

Almost every one of Brad's stories ended with the killer still on the loose in the woods. *These* woods. *Our* woods. And he insisted that every one of his tales was absolutely true.

Now, like I said, I was already scared enough being 300 miles from home, risking life and limb among the poison ivy, venomous snakes, grizzly bears, and disease-laden deer ticks that inhabited the wilds of northern Wisconsin. Add a constant stream of stories about 250-pound, one-armed, ax-wielding serial killers and you've got yourself one terrified camper.

The only thing that allowed me to sleep at night was the comforting reassurances of my roommate, Danny Olson. Danny was a soon-to-be seventh-grader from Madison whose dad was a real-life cop, so he was *very* skeptical about our counselor's so-called "true" stories of hook-handed madmen.

"Madison's a big town, and we don't have even 20 murders a year," Danny once explained. "Most involve people killing other people in their own families. You know, husbands killing wives. Wives killing husbands. The rest are mostly people killed during holdups and robberies, with some street-gang shootings thrown in. In fact, I've never heard my dad talk about even *one* murder involving a serial killer or homicidal maniac. And we have a state hospital for the criminally insane right across the lake from us in Madison."

"You do? Cool!" exclaimed Toby Resnick, a chunky 13-year-old from suburban Milwaukee. Toby always enjoyed Brad Hollman's campfire stories—the bloodier the better. Of course, he also turned into a blubbering bowl of jelly whenever he saw *real* blood, especially when it was his own.

"But Brad says all his stories are true," I noted, my hands nervously gripping the edge of my thin, lumpy mattress. "How could he make all that stuff up?"

"Just 'cause someone says something is true doesn't mean it is," Danny stated. "Brad just likes scaring kids. It makes him feel powerful or something. If I were you, I wouldn't believe anything he says."

What Danny said made sense. When I thought about it logically, how could all those homicidal maniacs be on the loose without there being any stories about them on TV or in the newspapers? And how could they all be living in the same forest? I mean, considering the number of stories Brad told us, these woods should be *crawling* with knife-wielding wackos. There should be enough of them to start their *own* summer camp!

So, in the days that followed, I began to view Brad's nightly campfire stories just a bit more critically. I started seeing them for what they were: exciting exercises of the imagination, no different from the horror movies I saw on TV back home. I started feeling better and even began enjoying Brad's twisted tales a little bit.

And then, toward the end of our third week of camp,

Brad showed up late at the nightly campfire wearing an uncharacteristic look of concern.

"No scary stories tonight, kids," he announced.

We all groaned in disappointment.

"What's the matter, Brad?" Danny Olson challenged. "Finally run out of old worn-out *Tales of Terror* ideas?"

"I can't tell you what's going on," Brad said nervously. "I'm just supposed to get you all back to your cabins. *Now.*"

"That's not fair!" Toby Resnick protested while chewing on a candy bar. "It's only nine o'clock. Lights-out isn't for another hour and a half!"

"I'm just doing what I'm told," Brad said, his voice cracking from nervousness. "Now get inside before we all get killed."

All 15 of us just stared at Brad blank-faced. What did he mean, before we all got *killed?*

"Who's going to kill us?" Danny asked calmly. *"You?"*

Brad seemed to be struggling with something for a few seconds, then he finally blurted it out. "All right, I'll tell you," he said, obviously happy to be relieving himself of a great burden. "Last May, a prisoner named Ethan Carter escaped from the Nebraska State Hospital for the Criminally Insane. The cops and the FBI have been looking for this guy for months, and finally he was spotted this afternoon just a few miles from here. The police are warning everyone in the area to stay inside with their doors closed."

"What kind of prisoner was he?" Toby asked, his eyes as wide as the cream-filled cupcakes he was preparing to eat next.

"Ethan Carter is a homicidal maniac," Brad replied.

"Supposedly he killed about 12 people throughout Nebraska and the Dakotas before he was arrested about a year ago."

"Yeah, right," Danny said with a sarcastic smirk. "Very funny. You think we're gonna fall for this?"

"I'm not making this up," Brad insisted. His voice quivered in a way I'd never heard before. For the first time ever, the guy seemed genuinely scared. "It's really happening."

"So if this Ethan Carter guy is for real, how come I've never heard of him?" Danny challenged. "My dad's a cop, you know."

"Carter's escape was only carried by the Nebraska papers," Brad explained. "I guess they never figured he'd make it all the way to Wisconsin."

Just then, a thunderlike rumble shook the night. We all turned just as two police helicopters, their searchlights blazing, roared over the nearby trees out toward Highway 18.

"The cops are looking for Carter right now," Brad said urgently. "Now let's get moving. I don't want to find one of you with an ax sticking out of your head."

He didn't have to ask twice. The next second I joined the other 14 boys in our group as we sprinted as fast as we could back to our cabins. The night reverberated with the sound of screen doors slapping closed, followed by the repeated *thunks* of wooden doors slamming shut. Within a minute, we were all safely inside, cowering beneath our coarse woolen blankets.

"You think this is for real?" I asked the others.

"You saw those police helicopters," Toby said. "When did they ever fly around here before?"

"I still think Brad's just trying to freak us out," Danny insisted. But as another police chopper drowned out Danny's voice, his assertion began to sound more like wishful thinking.

Now, I have to tell you, I was really starting to freak out. I'd never been the bravest of kids—until just a few years ago I would cry like a baby whenever the doctor gave me a shot—and the thought of being chopped to pieces by some schizo with a machete was nearly enough to make me wet my pants. I squeezed by eyes shut and tried to think "happy thoughts"—I pictured hot fudge sundaes, riding the roller coaster at Adventure World, and playing tennis with my dad—but the fantasies always ended with some crew-cut guy with a jagged scar across his forehead leaping out of the bushes and slicing me into bloody ribbons. I was glad it was so dark in the cabin that the other kids couldn't see the tears welling up in my eyes.

"I'm going to see what's going on," Danny suddenly announced, going to the door.

"Are you *crazy*?" I cried, choking back my tears. "He could be right outside with a sledgehammer ready to smash in your skull!"

"Oh, get real, Gary," Danny said. "Brad and the other counselors are probably sitting over in the mess hall laughing their heads off at us."

"If you're going over to the mess hall, could you bring me back a bag of chips?" Toby asked eagerly.

"No problem," Danny replied, then headed out into the night. I immediately jumped out of my bunk and slammed the door shut behind him. Danny may have been right—this could all be just some big practical joke—but I wasn't taking any chances.

About 15 minutes passed, and Danny still hadn't returned. With no word from anyone as to what was going on outside, our imaginations were starting to run wild.

"Maybe Carter's already slaughtered everyone in the camp, and we're the only ones left alive for miles," suggested Jason Gerzsky, a skinny redhead from the West Side of Chicago.

"Maybe Carter's coming for us right now with a machine gun," added Malcolm Green, a shy African American from Racine.

"I think we would have heard something if Carter was using a machine gun," I noted.

"Maybe it has a silencer," Malcolm countered.

Just then there was a knock at the door. *Thump! Thump! Thump!* We all bolted upright in our bunks as if hit by electric shocks.

"Who is it?" I croaked.

There was no reply. Cautiously, Toby slipped out of his bunk and headed for the door.

"What are you doing!?" I whispered in alarm. "That could be Carter!"

"I don't think a killer would knock," Toby replied. Then he opened the door.

Danny Olson was standing directly outside, the silvery moonlight giving his face an eerie ashen glow.

"Hey, Danny!" Toby said anxiously. "What's going on out there?"

He opened the screen door to let Danny come inside. But Danny didn't move. He just stood there, as still as a statue.

"Danny, are you all right?" I asked nervously.

Danny's lips twitched briefly, then he pitched forward and fell face-first into the cabin. We all rushed over and gasped in unison as we saw what we immediately recognized as a knife from the mess hall sticking out of Danny's back.

"Ahhhh!" I screamed.

"Ahhhh!" the others screamed in response.

Flinging aside any vestige of self-control, we began running around the tiny cabin like decapitated chickens, waving our arms and howling at the top of our lungs. Malcolm Green was the first kid to bolt out of the door, and we all immediately followed. We had no idea where we were going. All we could do was run around screaming like raving maniacs, perhaps believing that the sheer sight of four 12-year-old loons would send Ethan Carter scurrying off to wherever he came from.

The boys from two other cabins rushed out to see what all the commotion was about, and as soon as they saw Danny's body, they, too, joined our wild chorus.

"Tim Clemmons is dead!" another camper shouted as he ran over from the administration building, referring to one of the counselors. "All the other counselors are, too! Their bodies are all over the place!"

"Even Brad's?" I asked, trying to imagine our own counselor reduced to so much ground beef.

As if in response to my question, Brad suddenly staggered out from behind a clump of trees. Blood ran from an ugly gash on his right temple, and his eyes blazed with fear.

"We gotta get out of here," Brad grunted.

"How did you—?" I began, but Brad cut me off.

"I was on the CB radio talking to the police," he

wheezed, still trying to catch his breath. "They want everyone to get over to the old Oakbrook chemical factory down the road right away. They're using that as their command center."

Everyone at Camp Waupaca knew about Oakbrook. The only major industrial building for miles, it had gone out of business about 10 years earlier. It made sense for the police to use the building with its big, empty parking lot as their command center, but I had to wonder why they hadn't sent at least one policeman over to escort us. Maybe they were all busy trying to catch Ethan Carter.

Five minutes later, 15 of us were marching down State Route B, a narrow two-lane highway, toward the former factory. For the first time since this nightmare began, I was beginning to feel safe.

We arrived at the plant around midnight. Its big main building and chemical storage tanks loomed like black monsters against the star-filled sky.

"All right everyone, inside," Brad ordered as he held the plant's main door open for us. We hurried inside and found ourselves in a barnlike industrial building whose stairways, catwalks, and rusted work spaces were coated with a good half-inch of dust. The building was dimly lit by a few kerosene lamps hanging from the ceiling.

"So where are all the cops?" I asked when I realized that we were the only ones in the building.

"I don't know," Brad said as he slid the door shut with a resounding *bang*.

"Are you sure that was a real policeman you spoke to on the CB?" Malcolm asked anxiously. "Maybe it was Ethan Carter!"

"Let's get someplace safe," Brad said, looking nervously around the dark, empty plant. "Follow me."

Before any of us could respond, Brad started up a nearby metal staircase. The other campers followed. I waited until everyone else had gone and took my place at the end of the line. *Maybe Malcolm's right*, I thought. *Maybe Ethan Carter's setting us all up to be slaughtered!*

"All right, kids, gather around right here," Brad ordered, motioning us over onto a landing directly above a large open vat. The chemical smells here were awful, and my lungs were starting to burn.

"What's going on?" I finally demanded. "Who told you to bring us here? Where are the cops? And how did you get away from Ethan Carter when all the other counselors got killed?"

"I almost didn't get away," Brad said, wiping blood from his injured temple. "Tim Williams put up quite a fight—just before I cut his throat."

For what seemed an eternity, we all stood there in silent shock.

And then Toby finally shouted, "It's Ethan Carter!"

"Where?" Jason asked, spinning around in confusion.

"He's talking about Brad," I explained. "Brad Hollman *is* Ethan Carter! He's the one the cops have been looking for!"

"Very good, Gary," Brad—or should I say, the guy we knew as Brad—said with a wicked smile. "I was starting to think you'd never figure it out!"

Reaching into his back pocket, he pulled out a medium-size hunting knife with a large serrated blade. Its jagged teeth were coated with blood. Holding the knife in front of him, ready to strike out at the first kid who tried to move, he reached back for a large lever on the control panel behind him.

"What are you going to do?" I demanded.

"Kill you," Brad said with unnatural calm.

"But *why?*" I cried, my legs so shaky that I could barely stand upright.

"Because I'm a homicidal maniac," Brad replied matter-of-factly. "Hadn't you heard?"

With that, he pulled down on the lever. The huge barnlike factory reverberated with nearly two dozen death cries as the platform on which we were all standing suddenly tilted, sending us hurtling toward the huge vat of ancient acid waiting below.

My arms windmilled wildly as I struggled desperately to find some kind of handhold. Amazingly, just as I was about to slide into the vat of death, one of my belt loops caught on a jagged piece of rusty metal that protruded from the platform's grating. I hung there, eyes shut, listening to the screams of my friends as they fell into the acid bath, and feeling the hot sting of the burning liquid as it splashed onto my body. After about 15 seconds, the cries stopped. Before I passed out, I heard the laughter of Brad Hollman— alias Ethan Carter—as he walked off into the night.

$$\mathcal{T}\!\!\mathcal{T} \quad \mathcal{T}\!\!\mathcal{T} \quad \mathcal{T}\!\!\mathcal{T}$$

"Did they ever catch Brad Hollman?" a wide-eyed camper asked, the light of the campfire reflecting off his freckled face.

"No, they never did," 19-year-old Gary Welbeck replied gravely. "In fact, some say that he's still out here, still roaming these very woods, looking for more campers to slaughter."

The dozen campers who were gathered in front of their counselor took a collective gasp. And then one of them gave a cynical smirk.

"Yeah, right," he said. "You made this whole story up."

"Did I?" Gary said. He pulled back his right sleeve to reveal a large, purplish scar just below his elbow. "This is from the acid that splashed on me. I'll have to live with this for the rest of my life. Along with the nightmares." He looked into each of the campers' horror-filled faces, then smiled. "Well, that's it for tonight. Time to hit the hay. And pleasant dreams, kids."

Back in their cabin, the campers prepared themselves for bed.

"Do you think Gary's story was for real?" one of them asked.

"Oh, none of those campfire stories are ever real," the cynical one insisted. "The counselors just make them up to scare us. They think it's fun."

"Gee, I don't know," another 12-year-old said hesitantly. "That scar looked awfully real."

Just then, they heard a scratching sound at one of the windows. Instantly all the boys turned around in terror. For a brief second a few of them thought they saw a pair of eyes peering in through the glass, only to vanish a moment later. And others would later swear they heard maniacal laughter fading off into the dark, deep woods.

TEETH

><del>→ ◆ ◇ ◉ ◇ ◆ ←</del>

*I*T TOOK RESCUE WORKERS NEARLY 30 MINUTES TO *free the terrified 10-year-old from the machine. Although paramedics rushed the boy immediately to nearby County Hospital, it's now feared that the boy will lose his entire right foot as well as a portion of his leg below the knee."*

"Clarissa, it's time for dinner!" Mrs. Williams called from the kitchen.

But 14-year-old Clarissa didn't respond. She didn't even hear her mother's call. All of her attention was focused on the ghastly images on the TV in front of her. The blood, the torn flesh, the tears flowing down the injured boy's cheeks—they were enough to turn anyone's stomach. Clarissa could barely stand to watch it, but at the same time she was powerless to turn away. Something told her that this was more than just another story about someone being hurt in a freak accident. This was a warning. A danger sign. The boy being rushed to the hospital, his right foot chewed down to the bone, wasn't merely some nameless child from a distant part of town.

It was *her.*

⚡ ⚡ ⚡

"Clarissa, look up there!" Mona Phinston said excitedly, pointing to a storefront on the shopping mall's second floor. "Ambush is having a 20-percent-off sale on sweaters! Let's go!"

The tall redhead hurried toward the twin escalators about 30 yards down the crowded promenade. Clarissa, gripping the handle of her Unlimited Express shopping bag, immediately followed. Although the two 14-year-olds had arrived at the Parkside Mall just 20 minutes earlier, they had already managed to hit all five of their favorite fashion stores on the shopping center's lower level, and were now looking for fresh territory to conquer.

Both Clarissa and Mona took shopping very seriously. In fact, they tended to approach it much like a military campaign. They planned their attack strategy well in advance, establishing a clear set of objectives and a fixed timetable in which to complete them. As soon as they arrived at their "battlefield," they quickly surveyed the terrain, looking for any unexpected changes—such as unadvertised sales or store closings—that would force them to redefine their goals. They also made quick note of tactical considerations, such as particularly heavy crowds or mall redecorating, that might impede their progress. All of this took less than a minute. After that, they launched themselves into the fray, moving with the speed and confidence of experienced veterans.

Of course, all war is fluid, and even the best-laid plans have to be modified on the spot as new, unforeseen factors enter the equation. Such was the case with Ambush's sweater sale.

"Come on!" Mona shouted, waving her arms as she

hopped aboard the ascending escalator, "before all the good stuff is taken!"

Clarissa, just a few steps behind her friend, was about to step onto the escalator's moving stairs when she suddenly froze. A middle-aged woman, unprepared for Clarissa's abrupt halt, nearly slammed into her from behind.

"Oops, sorry," the woman said apologetically.

"Oh, it's all right," Clarissa mumbled, stepping aside. "Go ahead. I changed my mind."

The woman nodded a brief acknowledgment, then stepped aboard the escalator.

Shifting nervously from leg to leg, Clarissa forced her face into an uncomfortable smile as she watched her friend continue to ascend to the second floor. When Mona realized that she had arrived at the top alone, she hurried to the railing and looked down to see Clarissa still standing by the foot of the moving stairway.

"Come on!" Mona called cheerfully. "What are you waiting for?"

"I can't," Clarissa replied in a voice she knew was too low to be heard.

"What?" Mona called back.

"I *can't*," Clarissa hissed through clenched teeth. She looked up at Mona and shouted, "Don't move! I'll be right there!" She then turned and hurried back in the direction from which they'd come.

Mona stood by the rail watching incredulously as Clarissa ran to the marble staircase halfway down the mall's east wing, in front of the video-game boutique and frozen yogurt shop. Clarissa scrambled up the stairs with growing urgency, taking the last set two at a time. When she reached the landing, she spun around and sprinted back to Mona, who was staring at her as if Clarissa had lost her mind.

"What was *that* all about?" Mona asked, narrowing her eyes at her friend.

"I—ah—I just figured I needed the exercise," Clarissa said, tossing back her head and running her fingers through her long blond hair. "Now let's go check out those sweaters."

Ten minutes later the two girls emerged from Ambush carrying bags filled with what represented two whole weeks of baby-sitting income.

"Now *that* was a deal," Mona said, glowing with victory.

"I can't *wait* 'til Wendy Lee sees these," Clarissa added, admiring her new sweaters. Wendy was a fellow eighth-grader and rival for the title of World's Greatest Shopper.

"So how much money you got left?" Mona asked.

"About a buck-fifty," Clarissa replied.

"Want to get some frozen yogurt?" Mona suggested.

"Sure," Clarissa said, perking up. Together they headed for the nearby escalators. Again, Mona took the lead. And again, Clarissa stopped short just before stepping on.

"Clarissa?" Mona called, confusion in her voice, as she found herself dropping alone toward the ground floor.

"I'll meet you at the yogurt shop!" Clarissa called back, giving a tentative wave. Grabbing her shopping bags, she hurried back to the staircase, carefully watched her footing as she took the stairs step by step in her platform shoes, then stopped to catch her breath as she waited for Mona to rejoin her.

"All right, Clarissa, what the heck's going on here?" Mona demanded as she approached her friend.

"What do you mean?" Clarissa asked with an innocent cock of her head.

"I'm talking about the escalator," Mona said sternly. "That was twice you refused to go on."

"I told you, I need the exercise," Clarissa replied innocently. "I'm getting fat."

"You're five-foot-five and weigh 98 pounds," Mona recited from memory. "You lose any more weight and you'll disappear. Now seriously, what's your problem?"

"Well, *all right*," Clarissa moaned in exasperation. "It's just that, lately. . ." She hesitated.

"*Yeeeessss?*" Mona prodded.

"I've got this thing about escalators," Clarissa confessed. "They scare me."

Mona stared at her friend blankly.

"I'm serious," Clarissa whined, fidgeting uncomfortably. "Ever since I saw this story on TV, 'World's Scariest Machine Accidents: Part Four.'"

"Yeah, I saw that one," Mona nodded. "That boy got his pants leg caught in the escalator…"

"And it sucked him in up to his kneecap," Clarissa continued, her face twisted in disgust.

"And his sister tried to hit the emergency stop button," Mona went on with growing excitement.

"And meanwhile the boy was screaming and there was blood all over the place," Clarissa groaned, her face suddenly sickly pale. She gave an involuntary shudder.

"After I saw that, I had nightmares for a week. Then, last night on the news, there was another story about a kid getting caught in an escalator over at the Town & Country Mall in Hillside. It totally freaked me out. I was so scared, I couldn't even eat dinner!"

"So tell me, is it just escalators, or is it all mechanical conveyances?" Mona asked, trying to conceal a smile. "You know, elevators? Moving sidewalks?"

"Just escalators," Clarissa stated.

"Conveyor belts?" asked Mona.

"I told you, it's just escalators! Now leave me alone!" Clarissa snapped. She stiffened her body, then let out a long, measured breath. "Sorry. I'm fine now. Can we please get that yogurt?"

"You're sure you're fine with soft-serve machines?" Mona teased.

"You know, Mona," Clarissa said, "sometimes you are so lame."

茶 茶 茶

Clarissa was certain that her fear of escalators would soon pass. After all, she was experienced enough to know that just about *everything* she liked or disliked, loved or feared tended to change as she grew older. For example, there was a time when she absolutely hated broccoli. She couldn't even look at the green, treelike vegetable without feeling nauseated. But now she loved it. Back in fifth grade she thought the boy who sat next to her, Chris Paulsen, was a total geek. Now, in eighth grade, she thought he was darned cute. And then there was the time she was in love with the rock band Black Rain. Now she thought their music was boring. No doubt her fear of escalators, born from those graphic TV news accounts, would change, too.

But it didn't. At least not fast enough for Clarissa's tastes.

Two weeks after the incident with Mona, the two girls joined Wendy Lee and another friend from school, Hillary Davis, on another trip to the Parkside Mall. The trip represented another victory on the battlefield of material consumption until the girls' arrival at the west wing's escalator again stopped Clarissa's seemingly inexorable advance dead in its tracks.

"Come on, Clarissa," Wendy urged as she saw the girl staring at the escalator in dread. "What are you waiting for?"

"I—I'll meet you upstairs," Clarissa stammered, then immediately turned toward the distant staircase. Before she could move, Mona clamped a hand on her friend's shoulder.

"Don't do this, Clarissa," she hissed. "You're embarrassing me!"

"Just let me go," Clarissa ordered. "I'll be fine. I need the exercise."

"What's going on here?" Wendy inquired with obvious interest. "Clarissa, are you still scared of escalators?"

"Of course not!" Clarissa snapped back defensively. "Where did you hear that?" She immediately turned on Mona. "You told her, didn't you? How could you? Traitor!"

"It just came out in conversation," Mona replied with a pained smile.

"Well, for your information, Wendy, escalators are responsible for dozens of serious injuries every year," Clarissa said proudly. "Not to mention death through heart attacks, obesity, and other diseases directly linked to people's lack of exercise."

"Oh, get off it, Clarissa," Wendy scoffed. "You're a big scaredy-cat and that's all there is to it."

"I am *not* a scaredy-cat!" Clarissa said, wounded.

"Are too!" Wendy countered.

"Am not," Clarissa parried.

"Are too!" Wendy repeated.

"Hey, guys, chill out," Hillary said. "It's okay to be afraid of escalators. Just like my mom's afraid to fly and my brother's afraid of clowns."

"*I'm* afraid of clowns," Mona confessed. "Especially the kind who make balloon animals. They're creepy."

"Thank you, Hillary," said Clarissa. "Now, if you don't mind, I'll take the stairs."

"That might not be the best idea," Hillary stated. "My mom says that the best way to get over a phobia is to confront it head-on. The only way you're ever going to overcome your fear of escalators is to ride them."

"Hillary's right," Mona agreed. "There are dangers everywhere. When you cross the street, you could get hit by a bus. When you eat a burger, you could get food poisoning. The only way you're going to get through life is to accept the dangers and focus on the good stuff."

Clarissa tugged nervously on the colorful silk scarf around her neck. She knew her friends were right. This fear of escalators was not only making her a laughingstock, it was downright foolish. Millions of people rode escalators every day without a problem. The only reason that story about the mangled boy had been on TV was because it was so unusual. The chances that anything bad could happen to her on an escalator were infinitesimal.

"All right," Clarissa finally agreed. She steeled herself and fixed her eyes on the moving stairs in front of her. "Let's do it."

Her heart beating wildly, Clarissa marched forward, studied the speed at which the grooved stairs emerged from the base of the mechanism, then carefully timed her approach so that she stepped aboard with perfect fluidity. The sudden jolt of acceleration caught her slightly off guard, and she had to grip the rubber handrail to keep her balance.

"You're doing fine," Mona said as she stepped on behind Clarissa.

"Yeah, a real daredevil," Wendy added sarcastically.

They were already halfway up and Clarissa could feel herself relaxing. And why not? She'd ridden this thing countless times before seeing those stupid TV shows. Why should this time be any different?

Now she could see the grooved stairs beginning to compress and slide away beneath the comblike metal teeth at the very top of the escalator. She took a deep breath, released the handrail, took a step forward—and found herself stuck in place! Although her right leg was moving freely, her left felt as if it were being grabbed by a giant hand.

Clarissa looked down, alarmed. One of her shoelaces had come loose and had gotten snagged by the step's leading edge. It disappeared beneath the toothlike grid and was being pulled deeper and deeper—dragging her foot along with it.

"Help!" Clarissa screamed in panic. "I'm stuck!"

"Oh, cut it out!" Wendy scoffed as she stepped around Clarissa onto the second-floor landing. "Just pull your foot out."

"I can't!" Clarissa cried. Her shoe was now pressed up against the grid, and the mounting pressure on her foot was making it difficult for her to keep her balance. "Help me!"

"Get out of your shoe!" Hillary shouted as Mona grabbed one of her friend's flailing arms.

This was exactly what Clarissa was trying to do, but the tightening shoelace had pinned her foot in place, making it impossible for her to release herself.

"It's sucking me in!" Clarissa cried, tears running down her face. "Help me!"

"I've got it," Wendy shouted. She bent down and hit the big red emergency stop button between the two escalators. Immediately, the machine shuddered then came to an abrupt halt.

"I'll get your shoe out," Mona said, bending down to release the lace.

Moments later a uniformed mall security guard arrived, and within a minute Clarissa and her shoe were free.

"I *told* you this would happen!" Clarissa snapped at her friends.

"Clarissa, calm down," Mona said quietly.

"I am *not* going to calm down!" Clarissa continued at full tilt. "I could have been maimed for life on that thing! Or worse! I swear to you, I'm never going on an escalator again!"

"Fine, be that way," Wendy said, folding her arms. "I still think you're making a big deal over nothing."

"It wasn't *your* shoe that got caught," Clarissa said, tears still in her eyes.

"That's true," Wendy agreed. "I know enough to tie my shoes."

"That's it, I'm out of here," Clarissa said, grabbing her shopping bag.

"Where are you going?" Hillary asked as Clarissa stormed off down the corridor.

"Home!" Clarissa called back. "I'm all shopped out for today!"

A loud *ding!* caught her attention as, directly ahead of her, the mall's glass elevator arrived from the floor above. Determined to get back to the ground floor as quickly as possible, she stepped aboard.

The small elevator was already crowded with shoppers, so Clarissa had to squeeze her way in, where she found there wasn't even room to turn around. She was considering abandoning the elevator idea and taking the stairs instead when the doors slid shut behind her, locking her in.

Fine, she thought. *This'll be over in half a minute.*

Just then, she felt something grip her throat. Startled, she tried to turn around but found herself pinned against the door. In a split second her predicament became all too clear. The elevator doors had closed on the ends of her scarf, and it was tightening as the elevator descended. She was being choked to death!

Clarissa tried to scream, but it was impossible for her to get enough air. As the other passengers watched in mounting horror, she struggled frantically to free herself, but to no avail.

Just before she died, her eyes bulging wide in terror, a single thought ran through Clarissa's mind: *Dangers* are *everywhere . . . sometimes where we least expect them.*

MIRACLE DIET

≥⋯✦⋯⊖⋯✦⋯≤

IT'S NOT EASY BEING PERFECT. JUST ASK MIRANDA
Lawrence. As the star of the hit TV comedy series *Becky's
World*, the 14-year-old actress had to avoid anything that
could possibly blemish her image as the "All-American
Teenager." That meant her hair had to always be clean and
attractively styled. She had to always be seen in fashionable,
flattering clothes. She could *never* get a pimple. And she
could never, ever, under any circumstances, gain unsightly
extra weight.

"You're the idol of tens of millions of girls all over
the world," Marcy Dillard, executive producer and creator
of *Becky's World*, told her. "They all look up to you as a
symbol of the way a young teenager *should* be. Their loyalty
has made you a star, and it's up to you to be the role model
they demand."

But being "perfect" wasn't easy for Miranda.
Although the studio provided her with a professional stylist
to take care of her hair, an entire wardrobe department to
see that she wore only the hottest fashions, an award-
winning makeup artist to help keep her skin looking

flawless, and a personal trainer to supervise her exercise regimen, Miranda was still a normal teenager who got just as tired, lazy, and hungry as a girl who *didn't* have her own top 10 television show.

So when the season's last episode finished videotaping in late April, Miranda decided to throw caution to the wind and enjoy herself. She rented a secluded beach house north of Los Angeles for herself, her parents, and her big sister, Joanne, and together they had the most enjoyable summer vacation imaginable. Miranda slept until ten o'clock every morning. She spent her days lolling on the beach or hanging out with friends at an exclusive shopping mall. She went to movies. And she ate. Boy, did she eat. After nine months of virtually starving herself so she could look cute and petite, Miranda gorged herself on pizza, ice cream, cheeseburgers, and an incalculable number of chili fries.

But soon enough, early August arrived, and it was time for *Becky's World* to resume production. And when Executive Producer Marcy Dillard saw her star for the first time following the show's summer hiatus, the woman nearly had a heart attack.

"What *happened* to you?" Marcy cried, her eyes nearly popping out of her head. "You look so—so—*fat!!!*"

Actually, to anyone outside of Hollywood, Miranda Lawrence would have never been considered fat. Chubby, perhaps. Maybe even hefty, plump, or pudgy. But this was Tinseltown, a place built on creating impossible images, so to her producer's eyes, Miranda looked just slightly smaller than the Goodyear blimp.

"It's just a few pounds," Miranda insisted. "I'll

probably burn them off during rehearsals. Don't worry."

"My dear, you know the camera puts 10 pounds on a person," Marcy noted. "Add those to the 10 you really gained, and you'll photograph like a Thanksgiving Day parade float! No, no, no, this is totally unacceptable. We must take drastic action, and we have to do it *now!*"

"What kind of 'drastic action'?" Miranda asked warily.

"I'm putting you on a crash diet," Marcy stated. "You'll be restricted to 800 calories a day. And I'm going to have my own personal trainer work with you a minimum of six hours a day. Bruno is absolutely ruthless. You'll just adore him!"

Miranda imagined herself being worked out like a Marine recruit in basic training, and it scared her to death. And how could she possibly eat only 800 calories a day? There's almost that much in two slices of pizza! After bingeing all summer, going on a crash diet could kill her.

"What if I can't lose all my weight before shooting begins?" Miranda asked fearfully.

"Then I'm afraid we'll have no other choice," her producer replied soberly. "Becky will have an 'accident,' undergo plastic surgery, and return the following week with a brand-new face."

"You mean. . . ?" Miranda began, unable to finish her own sentence.

"You'll be fired," Marcy confirmed.

🌾 🌾 🌾

Terrified by the prospect of losing her job, Miranda discussed her dilemma with her friend Deborah Kerns, the frizzy redheaded girl who played the fictional Becky's best friend, Zoe. The two had been fast friends ever since they met at auditions 18 months earlier, and they were able to share even their deepest, darkest secrets.

"I don't know what I'm more scared of," Miranda confessed, "starving myself or losing my job. I wish they had a way for people to eat all they wanted without getting fat."

"Actually, they do," Deborah said. "My mom is an alternative nutritionist, and she has all kinds of holistic, drug-free products to help people stay thin naturally."

"Really? Why didn't you tell me this before!" Miranda asked.

"You were always so thin, I didn't think you *needed* to diet," Deborah replied.

"I was thin because I *did* diet!" Miranda cried. "And I hated every minute of it. Whatever your mother's got, I want some. Like, right now!"

"I'll see what I can dig up," Deborah promised. "I'm sure you'll love it."

☥ ☥ ☥

The next day Deborah joined Miranda in her trailer. Opening her purse, she pulled out a large red gelatin capsule.

"What's that?" Miranda asked.

"Mom's Miracle Diet," Deborah replied. "It's all natural. No drugs of any kind. You just take it with water, and you'll see results in days."

"You mean, I just have to take that one pill?" Miranda asked, somewhat confused.

"Yep," Deborah confirmed. "Just this one."

"What's in it?" Miranda inquired, increasingly skeptical.

"I can't tell you specifically. It's a secret," Deborah stated. "But I've taken these myself, and I can tell you, they work wonders, with absolutely no side effects. Mom says people used to take this stuff for centuries until modern medicine came along and spoiled everything."

"Well, I guess it's worth a shot," said Miranda, opening her palm to accept the capsule. "Anything beats starving myself."

Deborah handed her the capsule, then unscrewed a bottle of refrigerated bottled water. "Down the hatch," she said. Miranda popped the capsule into her mouth, threw her head back, and took several long swallows of spring water.

"Now what?" she said, gasping for air.

"Now enjoy yourself," Deborah replied. "The Miracle Diet will do the rest."

The next morning Miranda Lawrence woke up ravenously hungry. After showering and dressing herself as quickly as possible, she hurried down to the kitchen where she made herself two fried eggs, two sausage links, a bowl of cereal, and a warm buttered bagel.

"I thought Marcy put you on a diet," Joanne said as she stared at her little sister's lumberjack-sized breakfast.

"She did," Miranda replied through a full mouth. "But I don't need it any more. I'm on a new diet Deborah gave me."

"What kind of diet is *that?*" Joanne asked incredulously. "Eat so much that you *explode?*"

"Don't worry," Miranda assured her big sister. "I'm going to lose weight. Just watch."

Actually, Miranda couldn't for the life of her see how she could possibly lose even a pound eating like she was. But she had no choice. Since taking the big red diet pill, she'd become so hungry that if she didn't stuff her face with everything in sight, she'd be useless to anyone. She couldn't concentrate. She couldn't memorize her lines. She barely had enough strength to stand up. All she could think about was *food*.

But despite ingesting enough calories to power a small aircraft carrier, Miranda weighed herself the following morning and discovered that, miracle of miracles, she'd dropped an entire pound! The next morning the same thing occurred. Miranda ate and ate and ate, yet somehow managed to shed an average of one pound a day.

"You're looking absolutely marvelous!" Marcy Dillard told Miranda the day before they were scheduled to tape the new season's first episode. "I've seen the way you've been eating, and Bruno tells me you won't exercise. So, what's your secret?"

"Oh, no secret," Miranda said coyly. "I told you I'd burn off the fat during rehearsals. It's just nervous energy."

Two weeks after beginning her Miracle Diet, Miranda had dropped more than enough weight to satisfy Marcy and the show's other producers. In fact, by this point, they were starting to think she'd gotten *too* thin and asked her not to lose any more.

"So how do I stop losing weight?" Miranda asked Deborah when they were alone again in her trailer.

"Actually, that's the hard part," Deborah confessed. "It can be done, of course. It's just going to take a little work."

"Why? What was in that capsule, anyway?"

Miranda demanded. "I put it in my body. I think I have a right to know."

"Actually, it was a tapeworm," Deborah replied with a wan smile.

"A *what?*" Miranda cried, barely able to contain herself.

"A tapeworm," Deborah repeated. "It's a kind of parasite. It attaches itself to your intestines and feeds off the food you eat. People used to eat them to stay thin. The more you eat, the bigger and faster the tapeworm grows."

"*Big?* How *big?*" Miranda demanded, suddenly horrified by the prospect of some huge snakelike worm living in her stomach.

"I've heard that some tapeworms get as long as 10 or 12 feet," Deborah stated.

"10 or 12 feet!?" Miranda cried in horror, a wave of nausea rising into her throat.

"But you've only had yours for about two weeks, so I doubt it's more than two or three feet long," Deborah said offhandedly.

At this point it was all Miranda could do to keep from wrapping her fingers around Deborah's throat and throttling the girl to within an inch of her life. But she managed to control her violent urges and instead grabbed her friend's hand and looked her straight in the eye.

"I want it *out* of me, understand?" Miranda said, struggling to keep her voice under control. "And I want it out *now!*"

"No problem," Deborah said. "Come over to my house after work and we'll take care of it."

🜨 🜨 🜨

"All you have to do is swallow this," Deborah instructed. She showed Miranda what looked like a miniature wire birdcage tied to the end of a plastic fishing line.

"What is it?" Miranda inquired, studying the odd-looking device.

"It's a tapeworm trap," her friend explained. "I already put some food here." She indicated a bite-size piece of raw liver sitting inside the cage. "When the tapeworm goes for it, its head will get caught inside the wire mesh. Then we just pull it out."

"Pull it out through *where?*" Miranda asked, her face twisted in rising disgust.

"Your mouth," Deborah replied casually. "The same way it went in."

Miranda was absolutely sickened by what she was about to do but realized she had no other choice unless she planned to waste away to nothing. Bracing herself, she popped the inch-long worm trap into her mouth, filled her cheeks with water, then swallowed as hard as she could.

The cage hurt as it slowly worked its way down her esophagus. On more than one occasion she felt like throwing up, but she was able to suppress the gag reflex, and within a few minutes the pressure was relieved as the cage finally dropped into her stomach. It was an odd sensation having a fishing line running out of her mouth, and she shivered as she imagined how it would feel pulling the squirming tapeworm out of her gullet.

"Now what?" she asked Deborah, who held the free end of the line.

"Now we wait for a bite," her friend replied. "Just relax."

The two sat themselves down on Deborah's bed and turned on the TV. They were watching the beginning of a late-night talk show when Deborah perked up.

"I'm feeling something," she said tentatively, pulling on the fishing line. "I think we have a bite."

"Hurry!" Miranda cried. "Get it out!"

She clamped her eyes shut and opened her mouth wide. Deborah tugged and pulled this way and that, trying to ease the parasitic worm smoothly up through Miranda's throat. Miranda herself gagged repeatedly as she felt the line pulling on her insides.

And then—*snap!*

"What happened?" Miranda asked fearfully.

Deborah examined the frayed end of the filament. "I guess it broke the line," she replied, stating the obvious. "It must be bigger than I thought."

"So now I've got a tapeworm *and* a trap inside me!" Miranda howled, nearly in tears. "What am I supposed to do?"

"Well, tapeworms need food, just like we do," Deborah mused. "Maybe if you just cut off its food supply, it'll give up and leave on its own."

"But the only way to do that is to stop eating," Miranda noted. "And I took the tapeworm in the first place so I *could* eat!"

Deborah shrugged. "Hey, that's show business."

⚜ ⚜ ⚜

The next four days were absolute torture for Miranda Lawrence. Desperate to rid herself of the parasite, she virtually starved herself, ingesting only mineral water and vitamin pills. With the tapeworm continuing to draw on what nutrients it could find, Miranda quickly became tired and listless. She struggled into work every day at eight o'clock in the morning and worked until nine at night, with a four-hour break midday for tutored classes. During most of this rigorous schedule, it was all she could do just to stay awake.

And then, that Friday, just as they were preparing to shoot the week's episode in front of a live audience, Miranda realized that she could take this no more.

"I'll live with the darned tapeworm," she said to herself. "We'll be a team. Pals. Friends to the end. Just as long as I can eat!"

Desperate for food, she stumbled over to the craft services table, an area overflowing with snacks, drinks, and fresh fruit for the show's cast and crew. She reached for a big, luscious-looking piece of fresh carrot cake and took a deep, aromatic whiff. It smelled absolutely divine.

Her mouth literally salivating, she grabbed a fork and prepared to dig in.

Just then, she felt her throat tighten and her windpipe close off. She felt like she was choking, but that was impossible because she hadn't yet taken a bite.

Then she felt something moving in her mouth. It was hard and squirmy, like some sort of plated snake.

Panicking, she turned to her stage manager and pointed frantically to her mouth. The man's eyes widened in horror as he saw something emerge from Miranda's throat. Then a makeup girl screamed and dropped her cosmetics case as she, too, happened to glance Miranda's way.

Stumbling toward the makeup station, Miranda

looked into a mirror to see what was happening to her. What she saw filled her with such horror and revulsion, she wanted to scream herself, but with her windpipe choked off, all she could do was stare in wide-eyed terror.

The tapeworm, its segmented yellowish-red body topped with a squared-off head armed with a nasty set of clawlike pincers, was slowly working its way out of Miranda's mouth. No doubt attracted by the food at the craft services table, the starving parasite had decided to seek richer pastures, just as Deborah said it would.

But its timing couldn't have been worse. All around her, cast and crew members were running about in panic as they saw the monster worm, which must have been at least three feet long, wiggling out of the mouth of their star. The panic quickly spread to the audience who gasped in collective horror as they watched their "perfect teenage idol" expelling what looked like a snakelike alien from another planet.

Everything began to blur as Miranda's brain became starved for oxygen. The last thing she saw was the tapeworm, now more than half emerged, twisting back to stare its former host straight in the eye, before she dropped into unconsciousness.

杀 杀 杀

"That was such a stupid thing you did, Miranda," Marcy Dillard said as she sat on her young star's hospital bed. It had been two days since the paramedics brought Miranda here to the Burbank Medical Center where she was being treated for malnutrition. The doctors predicted that she would recover completely from her parasitic infestation.

"I know," Miranda confessed. "But I was desperate to lose weight. From now on, I'll do things the honest way. I'll watch what I eat. I'll exercise. And I won't take any more tapeworms."

"No, I mean it was stupid to barf the worm up in front of a live studio audience," Marcy said. She pulled out a copy of a tabloid newspaper called *Hollywood Insider* and showed it to Miranda. There was a picture of her on the cover with a huge tapeworm wriggling its way out of her mouth. The story was headlined BECKY'S MIRACLE DIET! LOSE TEN POUNDS A WEEK! "I told you, you're an idol for millions," the producer noted. "Do something and all your adoring fans will follow. So now, overnight, everyone in the country wants tapeworms! You've become the Princess of Parasites! What do you think about *that?*"

For the second time in as many days, Miranda Lawrence was completely speechless.

THE BODY

>─!─‹›─⊖─‹›─!─‹

NATE, SLOW DOWN," MATT POMEROY URGED HIS
16-year-old brother. "You're going too fast."

"I'm only going 50," Nate curtly replied, eyeing the
speedometer of his 1993 Japanese-built two-door coupe.
"The limit here is 45. You have to go at least 10 miles an
hour over the limit before the cops will stop you. And
besides, there are no cops on this road, anyway."

Matt looked at the road ahead, what little he could
see of it. They were in an area the locals liked to call "The
Boonies," a vast stretch of pine and cypress forest that was
as dark and foreboding as anything that could be found in
Central Florida. At night the woods formed a virtually
impenetrable wall of solid blackness that often caused
motorists here on Highway 178 to lose all sense of
perspective. The woods also made it all but impossible for
cops to hide in waiting, looking for passing speeders, since
there was virtually no room to conceal a patrol car.

Nate's probably right, Matt thought. *No one's going to
stop us for speeding.*

The fact was, Matt's brother, Nate, had been driving

for more than eight months, and so far he hadn't gotten so much as a parking ticket. He was generally a careful, courteous driver who seemed to know his way around the local roads, so Matt, who wouldn't be driving for another two years, felt safe with him. Still, out on the twisting rural highways outside of their hometown of Winter Lake, Florida, Matt couldn't help but get a little nervous. He tugged on his shoulder harness, making sure it was firmly in place. He scanned the dashboard directly in front of him, secretly wishing the manufacturer had had the foresight to install passenger-side airbags in its 1993 models. Not that he expected his big brother to get them into a head-on collision, but on these roads, anything was possible.

"So, how'd you like the movie?" Matt asked, referring to the action film they'd seen earlier that evening at the multiplex in nearby Long Creek.

"It was okay," Nate said with a shrug. It was difficult to get Nate to admit to liking anything. To show any enthusiasm would be very uncool. "Let's get some music on in here."

He reached over for the in-dash radio, only to have his younger brother get there first.

"I got it," Matt said, hitting the power button. "You keep both hands on the wheel." A moment later the interior of the car thudded with the sounds of rap music.

"You are such a wuss," Nate scoffed. "What do you think I'm gonna do? Lose control?"

Smiling wickedly, Nate jerked the wheel to the left, momentarily skidding over into the oncoming lane.

"Don't do that!" Matt snapped.

"I've been driving for over six months. I'm a pro," Nate assured his brother, now snapping the wheel from side to side. His right foot gently pressed down on the accelerator, increasing their speed to 55 miles per hour.

"I'm sorry," Matt said, struggling to control his anger. He hoped that by acquiescing to his brother, he'd get Nate to stop acting like an idiot.

"You'd better be," Nate said, slightly easing his foot off the accelerator. "I've got two and a half years on you. Always will. It's time you showed me some respect."

Matt sat back and gave a long, measured sigh as he watched the car settle back into the middle of their lane at a swift but still comfortable speed. The air was warm and heavy with humidity, and he enjoyed the feeling of the moist wind from his open window on his face.

Just then, something darted into the road about 50 feet in front of them.

"Look out!" Matt screamed, instinctively bracing himself for an impact.

Nate's reflexes were fast, but not fast enough—not at the speed they were traveling. He'd barely gotten his foot on the brake when—*thump!* Something struck their right front fender, causing the car to buck under the impact. Matt hung on for dear life as the car skidded to a stop with a ear-splitting *screeeeeeech!*

They were a good 50 yards from the point of impact when the car finally came to a rest on the road's gravel shoulder. Matt and Nate sat in stunned silence for several seconds, breathing deeply and silently making sure that they were both in one piece.

"What the heck was *that?*" Nate finally asked.

"I don't know," Matt said. "It looked like a little kid." Although he'd barely caught a glimpse of the figure as it dashed out in front of their headlights, Matt was certain that it was human in form, perhaps somewhere between three and four feet tall.

"It wasn't my fault," Nate said, clutching the steering wheel. Matt could just imagine the horrible things that must be going through his brother's mind. He'd just killed a child. Even if it was an accident, he'd have to deal with that for the rest of his life. Not to mention the police, and maybe losing his license. Matt himself knew he'd be having nightmares about this night for as long as he lived.

"We've got to check it out," Matt insisted. "Maybe he's still alive. Or maybe it wasn't a kid at all. Maybe it was some kind of animal."

This last possibility seemed to break Nate out of his trance. If they'd only struck an animal, then they could go home guilt-free. After all, people here in Central Florida hit animals in the highways all the time, especially the possums and armadillos that were forever dashing blindly across even the busiest of highways.

"All right," Nate agreed, and he put the gear shift into reverse. Matt turned around and watched as they slowly rolled back in the direction from which they'd come. At the same time, he kept a sharp eye out for any oncoming traffic. The last thing they needed was another collision, but so far the highway appeared totally deserted.

Nate braked the car and turned off the ignition, but he kept the lights on to help illuminate the immediate area. Without a word, the two brothers then stepped out of the car and walked slowly toward what appeared to be a small body lying crumpled against the trunk of a tall cypress tree.

Matt could see the beginning of Nate's skid marks about 30 feet farther up the road. From the looks of things, the car had struck this guy—if it *was* a guy—with such force that it had knocked him a good 10 yards through the air.

"Look at that," Nate said, his face twisting in a combination of confusion and disgust. "Is that a person?"

Matt crept to within 10 feet of the body. Although it was difficult to make out details in the reddish glow of their car's taillights, it was clear that this was not a normal child.

Although it had a humanlike shape, its head, now twisted to one side, was unusually small in comparison to its body, which was thicker and more barrel-like than a person's. Also, its arms were curiously long, while its legs were shorter than one might expect. Most unusual of all, the body appeared to be covered in thick, reddish brown hair.

"You know what I think?" Nate said, now finding the courage to come within just a few feet of his unwitting victim. "I think it's a monkey."

"It's not a monkey," Matt corrected him. "It's an ape."

"Same thing," Nate scoffed.

"No, it's not," Matt insisted. "Monkeys have tails. Apes don't. This is an ape. I think it's an orangutan."

"Yeah, I remember seeing one of these guys in the Olagapocka Zoo," Nate agreed, referring to a small zoo situated just about five miles from where they stood. "Hey, you think maybe this guy's from there?"

"Makes sense to me," Matt said. "Not a lot of people

around here have orangutans. It probably escaped and has been running through the woods looking for food. Hey, I bet there's a reward. Maybe we can make some money by turning it in."

"Make money by turning in a *dead* orangutan? I don't think so," Nate said. "Especially when *we're* the ones who killed it."

"What do you mean *we?*" Matt challenged. "You were the one who was driving."

"Well, you were the one who was messing with the radio," Nate shot back. "If you hadn't been fooling around, I could have kept my eye on the road."

"Hey, don't blame this on *me!*" Matt shouted. "You're the driver, the captain of the ship. Whatever happens is *your* responsibility."

Nate just stood in silence for a few moments, his eyes fixated on the dead ape. It may not have been a person, but it was still humanlike enough for its death to engender uncomfortable feelings of sympathy and revulsion in both the boys.

"I think we should just get out of here," Matt finally stated. "Let someone else take care of this."

He was starting back for the car when his brother shot out a hand. "Wait," Nate said. "I still think there's a way we can make some money off this."

"You said it yourself, Nate. No one's going to pay money for a dead ape," Matt insisted.

"But what if we don't say it's an ape?" Nate proposed, his eyes twinkling mischievously. "What if we say it's something else?"

"What the heck are you talking about?" Matt

demanded, suddenly getting a very uncomfortable feeling.

"Don't say no before I'm finished talking," Nate said, then went on to detail the most outlandish plan Matt had ever heard.

🜚 🜚 🜚

The *International Star Bulletin* wasn't the most famous tabloid newspaper in America. It didn't have the highest circulation and it certainly didn't pay as much for its stories as many of the other "rags" that could be found at supermarket checkout stands from coast to coast.

But the *International Star Bulletin* did have one advantage the other, better-known tabloids didn't: It was headquartered in the Pomeroys' hometown of Winter Lake, Florida.

It was well known among the town's residents that the editors of the *Star Bulletin* would pay anywhere from $100 to $1,000 for stories and photos they could run in the paper. And the more outrageous, the better. One local farmer had pocketed $500 for a photo of a two-headed snake. A barber had once gotten $250 for a story about how the pain in his fingers could predict the weather. A local "psychic" had walked off with a cool $500 for proclaiming that the world would end on Arbor Day, 1995. Fortunately, the paper didn't ask for a refund when the planet failed to be destroyed.

It wasn't difficult for Matt and Nate to speak to one of the *Star Bulletin's* reporters. They merely walked up to the front desk and said they had a one-of-a-kind photo to offer. They were immediately ushered to the cluttered cubicle of a young, sandy brown-haired woman named Brenda Tyrell.

"Okay, boys, what have you got?" Brenda asked as she sipped coffee from a ceramic Elvis mug.

Looking dead serious, Nate reached into a large manila envelope and extracted an eight-by-ten black-and-white photo. Brenda nearly gagged on her coffee when she saw the picture.

"What the heck is *that?*" she gasped.

"An alien," Matt replied, struggling to maintain a deadly grim expression. He glanced over at the photo they'd just presented. The subject certainly *looked* like an alien. It was small, hairless, and only somewhat human-looking. In fact, it was the orangutan Matt and his brother had accidentally killed the previous night. They had shaved off all its fur and covered it with gray spray paint.

"We were driving down Highway 178 when we saw this weird light in the sky," Nate began. He then went on to relate a hair-raising tale of seeing a flying saucer land, followed by their near-abduction by a half-dozen small gray-colored aliens, and how one of the aliens had died when Nate had been able to break free and hit it over the head with a rock.

"So where's the body now?" Brenda asked eagerly, obviously knowing a good yarn when she heard one.

"It melted," Matt replied. The brothers both knew that the ape's body would be recognized for what it was if allowed to be inspected by an even halfway-competent zoologist, and so agreed that they'd be better off if the "alien" had simply "disappeared." "We took the body home and took this picture, and right after that it dissolved into dust," he explained.

In reality, they'd taken the corpse to the Winter

Lake landfill, where it was now buried beneath countless tons of trash.

"Too bad," Brenda said, now tilting the picture from side to side. "It's a good story. Pretty good picture, too. You kids build this thing yourself?"

"Build what *thing?*" Nate asked.

"This mannequin. This doll. Whatever it is," Brenda explained. "I mean, come on. We all know it's not really an alien . . ."

"It's not a doll," Matt insisted. "It's real. It was alive."

"Yeah, fine, whatever you say, kids," Brenda said with a weary sigh. "Tell you what. I'll talk to my editor about this. I think we can manage to find, oh, $500 for you? That's for both the photo *and* your story."

Nate and Matt looked at each other in shock. Five hundred dollars! That would give them $250 each! They'd be rich!

"Deal," they said in unison.

⚸ ⚸ ⚸

Matt and Nate's parents had gone out for dinner, leaving the boys to fend for themselves on this unusually dreary Friday night. It had been nearly a full week since their story and photo had appeared in the *International Star Bulletin*, and the teasing phone calls from friends and relatives had finally begun to subside.

"I wonder if we did the right thing," Matt said as he and his brother sat in front of the family's big-screen TV watching a brainless cop show.

"Are you kidding?" Nate scoffed. "We're 500 bucks richer. How could that be wrong?"

"Well, the guys at the zoo are probably still

wondering what happened to their orangutan," Matt noted. They'd seen a story about the missing ape on the local news the same day they'd sold their story to the *Star Bulletin*. A $1,000 reward was being offered—but only if the primate was found alive. "At least we should have dropped them an anonymous note or something, telling them that we'd killed it on the highway. It *was* an accident, you know. They couldn't put us in jail or anything."

"I don't know," Nate said warily. "There's probably some law against shaving dead apes in this state. The best thing we can do is shut up about what happened. After all, what they don't know can't hurt us." Just then, the picture on the television burst into formless static.

"Hey, what's going on?" Nate said, hitting buttons at random on the remote control.

"The cable must be out," Matt surmised.

The next moment all the lights in the room began to flicker on and off, and the air was filled with an unearthly buzzing sound. The air seemed to be electrified. Matt could feel the hairs on the back of his neck stand on end.

"Matt, look outside!" Nate shouted, pointing out the family room's glass sliding door. At first Matt thought that an airplane, its landing lights ablaze, was about to crash into their backyard. But as he watched in awe, the brilliantly lit object slowed and settled featherlike onto the grass.

"Nate—" Matt began, but his words were choked off as his body suddenly became immobile. He wanted to move, to run to the phone and call the police, but some unseen force was pinning him to his chair.

As he watched in rising terror, three small grayish figures appeared at the window. They stood about four feet tall and had small oblong heads and long arms that terminated in large apelike hands.

"Where is he?" Matt heard a voice scream into his mind.

"Wh-where is *who?*" Matt managed to stammer in reply.

"Our crewmate," the telepathic voice demanded. "He was lost in this area of your planet 15 day cycles ago. Give him to us or die."

"That wasn't really an alien," Nate insisted as the figures pressed themselves against the glass. "It was an ape. We just shaved its body. It was a joke . . ."

"'Joke'?" the alien voice repeated. "What is the meaning of 'joke'?"

Matt could see the aliens' eyes now. They were big, black, and soulless, like the eyes of an insect. Their mouths were thin, lipless slits set above small, sharp chins.

And they weren't laughing.

THAT EXTRA MILE

>──I──◆──⊙──◆──I──<

MY NAME IS FLYNN BRODERICK. OR, AT LEAST IT *WAS* Flynn Broderick. I say *was* because I'm dead. If you want to know what it's like being dead, well, I don't recommend it. And I particularly don't advise dying the way *I* did.

Let me start at the beginning.

At the time of my untimely demise, I was about to graduate from Ramona Junior High School in Daytona Beach, Florida. I was a good student. Better than most. I always got A's on my report card. One or two B's. Never a C, D, or, heaven forbid, an F. But my homeroom teacher, Mrs. Barr, still gave me a hard time.

"You're a very bright girl, Flynn. *Very* bright," she'd always say to me. "You could be a top student. But you don't try hard enough. You don't go that extra mile."

"That extra mile." Mrs. Barr just *loved* that expression. What she meant was, even though a score of 95 on a history test was an A, why not go for a solid 100? And if you could score 100, why not make it 110 with a little extra credit? Personally, I found this really irritating. I mean, an A is an A is an A, so what difference does the actual score make? In fact, it doesn't make sense to do more work than you have to. Like, if you're riding your bike from your house to the mall, what's the point in riding a mile farther on? It kind of defeats the purpose, doesn't it?

My best friend, Hillary Tyson, agreed with me. In fact, she thought Mrs. Barr should be kissing my feet instead of criticizing me all the time. Hillary, you see, was not the sharpest knife in the kitchen drawer. Although she came from a very rich family and was very good-looking and very, very popular, she had to struggle like crazy just to score C's on her tests. A B was cause for celebration. Her mom and dad did everything they could to help her. They hired private tutors. They sent her to special "learning centers." Nothing seemed to help. Apparently, on the day they were handing out brains, Hillary Tyson was out shopping.

"I think you're a genius," Hillary told me over lunch after one of our teacher's "extra mile" speeches. "If I had just half your brains, I'd be happy. Mrs. Barr's crazy for giving you such a hard time. I mean, who does she want you to be? Alfred Einstein?"

"That's *Albert*," I corrected her.

"Where?" she asked, looking behind her.

"Einstein," I patiently explained. "His name was *Albert* Einstein, not Alfred."

"There. That's what I'm talking about," Hillary said emphatically. "You're *so* smart. I bet someday you'll win one of those Noble Prizes."

"No-*bel*," I almost said but decided to keep my mouth shut. Hillary's point was well taken; who cared if she got the details wrong?

Anyway, this went on for most of the year. I'd take

my tests, get my 94s and 96s, and Mrs. Barr would say things like, "You're so smart. You could do so much better if you'd just slow down;" "Good enough *isn't*;" and, of course, "You should go that extra mile."

After a while her criticisms just became so much background noise. I was having fun in school, getting good grades with only a minimal amount of work, and the last thing I wanted to be was one of those four-eyed Poindexters who spent all of their precious youth huddled in the library so that, should they ever be asked, they could recite the name of every U.S. president and vice president in reverse alphabetical order. After all, I had a life.

This included hanging out with Hillary Tyson at her place on the marina. Like I said earlier, Hillary's dad was rich. Rich enough to own a six-bedroom waterfront house, a 50-foot yacht, three German luxury cars, his own twin-engine airplane, and a high-definition television that you could only buy in Japan. Owning two successful auto dealerships can do that for a person.

About a month before school let out, Hillary and I were sunning ourselves on the wood deck of their private pier when I had a brilliant idea.

"Hey, Hillary, how about we have our graduation party here?" I suggested. "This is a great party house. You've got all that room inside, plus the deck here. And the hot tub. We could even go sailing."

"That is a good idea," Hillary agreed. "I'm sure my mom and dad would say yes. They always say they'd rather have me here at home instead of at a party somewhere else where they don't know *what* the heck I'm doing. Boy, I wonder why I didn't think of that!"

"That's what you have *me* for," I said smugly.

Hillary didn't disagree.

Looking back, I wish she had.

That evening Hillary and I worked up our invitation list. There were a total of 28 people in our homeroom class. A good half of them were total losers—geeks, nerds, punks, blimps, and the hygienically challenged—who we were able to eliminate immediately. That left a total of six kids on our A-list—the cool kids we absolutely *had* to invite—and another seven who were on our B-list—kids we'd have over just to fill up the house. After all, it *was* a pretty big place.

Then there were our friends from other elective classes—math, science, gym, art, and music. That brought the grand total up to 30, divided almost evenly between boys and girls. Looking the list over, I couldn't help but feel a surge of pride. It was a true work of art.

Hillary was right about her mom and dad. They were happy to host the graduation party. They figured, that way, their daughter would stay out of trouble. They were so pleased with the plan they even gave us permission to take out their two smaller sailboats.

The party was scheduled for the Saturday before graduation. The weatherman said we'd have partly cloudy skies, with a high in the low 80s. And the morning dawned just as predicted. But as the time for the party approached, the sun disappeared, the wind kicked up, and the skies began to look awfully threatening.

"Don't worry about it," Hillary said as she set a bowl of cheese popcorn out on the long snack table in her dining room. "They said it wasn't going to rain and I believe them. Nothing is going to spoil this party—not even the weather."

Something about those clouds made my blood run cold. It was probably a signal for me to grab my things and run as far away from that house as I could. But it was a warning I chose to ignore.

The first of our friends showed up around two o'clock, and by three the party was in full swing. Music blasted from the Tysons' mammoth stereo system, kids feasted on everything from pizza puffs to mini-tacos, and enough soft drinks were consumed to float the family yacht.

Hey, I may not have given my best effort in school, but when it came to throwing parties, I always put out 110 percent.

Around four-thirty, Hillary suggested that we all go sailing.

"Great idea!" I said, grabbing a can of diet cola and heading straight for the pier. I'd always loved the water. It gave me a sense of power and freedom I hadn't been able to find anywhere else. But being from a normal middle-class family, I rarely had a chance to go out on a private boat. Thank goodness for Hillary. Her family had not one, but two 10-foot sailboats, and Hillary was always happy to take me out whenever I asked.

In fact, thanks to Hillary, I'd become something of a sailor myself. I knew how to set a sail, and how to tack into the wind. I wasn't going to win any races, but I could get a sailboat from point A to point B with a good amount of style and grace.

Or so I thought.

"Be careful out there, kids," Mrs. Tyson called as we all thundered out onto the pier. "The weather's looking a little nasty."

"We'll be fine, Mom," Hillary insisted as she handed bright orange life vests to everyone who wanted to sail. "We'll stay close to the shore."

Famous last words.

I was one of the first kids on a boat. I chose my favorite, a sleek little blue number with the name *Porpoise* painted on its stern. I settled back, grabbed hold of the rudder, and prepared to make way. I was soon joined by two more friends, Randi Kramer, a small, thin-boned eighth-grader with high cheekbones and dyed jet-black hair, and Samantha "Sam" Albright, a tall junior varsity basketball player whose hair looked like a frizzy blond steel-wool pad.

"Are you sure you know how to drive this thing?" Sam asked nervously, clutching the sides of the boat so tight I thought she was going to break off a chunk of fiberglass.

"You don't *drive* a boat, you *sail* it," I corrected her. "And, yes, I've done this a few times."

"Do we really have to wear these stupid things?" Randi asked, indicating her bulky life jacket. "They look so dorky. Besides, if it's my time to die, I don't see the point in fighting it." Randi always did have a rather dark view of things.

"Keep it on!" Hillary shouted from another boat as she and two other friends drifted away from shore. "Hey, Flynn, I'll race you to the breakwater!"

"You're on!" I shouted back.

We cast off and soon were slicing our way across the increasingly choppy waters toward the row of granite boulders that comprised the breakwater. Already the temperature had dropped a good 10 degrees, and the wind had kicked up considerably. I looked up just in time to see the hazy sun become totally blocked out by a mean-looking storm cloud. There was no doubt about it—the weather was turning ugly. But I wasn't going to let a little low-pressure system spoil my good time. I was determined to have fun, even if it killed me.

"Beat ya!" Hillary shouted triumphantly as she turned her boat around at the base of the breakwater. She had beaten me by a good 15 seconds, aided no doubt by the fact that she'd actually taken lessons in this sport. "Now I'll race you back!"

"I'm going to the end of the breakwater!" I called back.

"You know we're not allowed to leave the harbor!" Hillary warned me. It was a rule I'd been told every time we'd gone boating. Mr. and Mrs. Tyson felt fine about us sailing around the protected waters of the harbor. Even in the worst weather, the waves here inside the breakwater were relatively small and the currents were easily manageable. Outside the harbor, out on the open ocean, it was a very different story. As soon as you got beyond the breakwater, the sea took charge. You could immediately feel the waves surge beneath you, and the current become swift and powerful. Even the wind seemed stronger and less predictable. As capable a sailor as Hillary was, her folks still weren't comfortable with her sailing alone on such waters, and especially not with an inexperienced landlubber like me along.

I had no intention of breaking the Tysons' rules, but I saw no reason why I couldn't at least *bend* them a little. There was no law against going to the *mouth* of the harbor, of going as far as I could without actually venturing out onto the open sea. After all, just because a person goes to look over the edge of a cliff doesn't mean she's actually going to jump.

"I think we should be heading back," Sam said nervously as the breakwater's opening came into view. Beyond were the surging waves of the great Atlantic Ocean.

"In a minute," I stated, adjusting the sail in an attempt to hold a steady position.

Just then, a cold, wet wind whipped in from behind us. It caught me off guard, and before I knew what was happening, we were slicing our way out past the breakwater and onto the open sea.

"Turn around!" I heard Hillary shout from somewhere behind me.

"I'm trying!" I yelled back as I struggled with the sail and rudder. But the tide was going out, and between the channel's strong current and the fierce storm winds coming in from the west, there was nothing I could do to change course. Try as I might to control it, our tiny sailboat moved farther and farther away from the safety of the breakwater.

"Look out!" Sam cried, pointing off to starboard. A large cabin cruiser was bearing straight down on us, its captain obviously eager to get into the harbor ahead of the approaching storm. If it maintained its present course, it would slice directly into us.

"Stop!" Randi shouted, waving her arms toward the oncoming boat. "Don't hit us!" She jumped to her feet in an attempt to signal the captain.

"Sit down!" I screamed, knowing that, by standing, Randi was throwing our small, fragile craft horribly off balance.

Just then, the air reverberated with the shrill blast of the cabin cruiser's air horn. Just 30 feet away from us, the boat veered sharply to the right. For a moment, I breathed a sigh of relief as I realized that we weren't going to crash. But my joy turned to terror as I saw that the cruiser's abrupt maneuver had kicked up a huge wave, and it was rushing straight for us!

Before I could do anything, the wave smashed into us broadside. Randi, who was still on her feet, was immediately thrown overboard. Sam screamed and reached over to grab her. At the same time our tiny boat tipped sideways as it was carried up and over by the wave, and the next thing I knew I was thrashing about in the cold salt water.

"Sam! Randi!" I called, struggling to get my bearings.

"Right here!" Randi shouted. I looked over my shoulder and saw my friends bobbing on the water's surface like red-vested corks as they clung desperately to the capsized boat. I thanked the heavens we hadn't given in to impulse and removed our life jackets. They had probably just saved our lives.

"What do we do now?" Sam asked, obviously terrified. "Are we going to die?"

"We're not going to die," Randi insisted. "We're not too far out yet. We can try to swim back to the breakwater."

"Are you crazy?" I asked in disbelief.

"It's less than a mile," Randi said, gesturing to the slowly receding line of boulders. "We've all swum that far in gym class."

"But not in open water," I noted.

"We have our life preservers," Randi said. "We're not going to drown. It'll just take some effort, that's all."

"Go knock yourself out," I said sarcastically. "I'm staying with the boat. The Coast Guard will find us soon enough."

"I'm not waiting around," Randi said. "I'll send someone out to get you."

And with that, she pushed herself away from the boat and began swimming with strong, measured strokes toward shore.

"Wait for me!" Sam shouted, then began swimming away as well.

I couldn't for the life of me understand why they were doing this. The boat was still intact and, although capsized, was in no danger of sinking. All anyone had to do was hold on and wait for help to arrive. To take the kind of chance they were undertaking seemed to me to be absolutely insane.

But as I watched their red life jackets grow smaller and smaller, I couldn't help but think about what Mrs. Barr had been saying to me all year. I just was too complacent. I opted for whatever path offered the least resistance. I avoided expending any unnecessary energy, refusing to go "that extra mile."

As the line of the breakwater grew smaller and smaller, and as a cold, stinging rain began to pelt my face, I silently cursed myself for not going with Sam and Randi, for not having the courage to take the kind of risk they were more than ready to accept. They were probably almost to shore by now.

My frustration then turned to fear as I caught a flash of movement out of the corner of my eye. Turning, I saw the chilling shape of a triangular dorsal fin slicing through the waves not 10 feet away from me.

Even if the Coast Guard did eventually come looking for me, they were going to be too late. I had company now.

Sharks.

WILL-O'-THE-WISP

><·—·‹•›·—·⊙·—·‹•›·—·‹<

WHAT'S THAT WEIRD LIGHT?" 14-YEAR-OLD TORY Brand asked as she gazed out at the nearby woods.

"What light?" her cousin Erin asked, joining her at the living room window.

"There. Out in the trees," Tory said. She pointed toward the thick forest that began just 10 feet beyond her cousin's expansive backyard. Although it was late spring, the oak, elm, birch, and cottonwood trees that populated much of the area were still as stark and barren as they'd been all winter. As depressing as this looked in the daylight, at night it was downright creepy. The house appeared to be surrounded by an army of twisted giants, their huge, skeletal limbs poised to strike at any moment.

The eerie atmosphere was now heightened by the appearance of a soft orange light that appeared to flicker and dance among the distant trees. Too unfocused to be a flashlight, too bright for a candle flame, the light hovered in place for several seconds, then winked out and appeared hundreds of feet away.

Tory watched the strange light in fascination. She

couldn't help but get the feeling that this was more than just some weird optical illusion or random phenomenon. She was sure that the light was somehow *alive.*

"Do you see it, Erin?" Tory asked eagerly.

"I sure do," her cousin confirmed. Tory and Erin were the same age, born just two months apart, and shared their family's characteristic long oval face, sharp chin, bright green eyes, and long, sandy blond hair. Many people thought they were sisters, but despite outward appearance, the girls couldn't be more different.

Erin, who lived here outside the city of Ann Arbor, was a quiet, conservative girl who enjoyed familiar routines and avoided physical risk. Tory, on the other hand, was an adventurer who loved exploring the great outdoors. She took full advantage of the recreational activities available in Eugene, Oregon, where she lived with her parents and two brothers, and until now had found her visit to her cousin's house to be rather boring. In fact, the appearance of this weird, unearthly light was the first excitement she'd experienced all week.

"What do you think it is?" Tory asked. "It almost looks like a ghost."

"I've seen it before," Erin replied. "People around here call it 'Will-o'-the-Wisp.'"

"What?" Tory asked, unfamiliar with the term.

"Will-o'-the-Wisp," Erin repeated. "This weird light shows up every once in a while, especially in the spring."

"What do you think it is?" Tory asked, her eyes still glued to the light dancing playfully among the distant trees.

"Well, I've heard a few explanations," Erin stated. "The first is that it's swamp gas."

"Swamp gas?"

"In autumn, all the leaves fall off the trees, collect on the ground, and start to decay," Erin explained. "When we have a lot of snow, like we did last winter, the leaves get trapped for a long time. As they rot, they release all kinds of gases, like methane. Then when the snow finally melts, these pockets of methane make their way to the surface and ignite by themselves."

"You said there was another explanation. What is it?" asked Tory. She was unsatisfied with such a boring scientific answer for such a strange and beautiful thing.

"Well, about 50 years ago, a girl was out playing in those woods when she got trapped in a pit of quicksand," Erin said.

"You have quicksand around here?" Tory asked in surprise. She turned away from the window and looked at her cousin with mounting interest.

"It shows up now and then," Erin confirmed. "Anyway, the girl died, and some of the kids around here say that every few months or so, her ghost shows up looking for someone to play with."

"Cool," Tory said, turning her attention back to the forest. Now *this* was a story she liked.

"Personally, I think it's just swamp gas," Erin said flatly. "I certainly don't believe in ghosts."

"You wouldn't," Tory mumbled, still fascinated by the nocturnal light show. Just then, the light winked out. Seconds passed, but the forest remained dark.

"Show's over," Erin said, turning away from the living room. "Maybe it'll come back tomorrow night. It's usually there for a few days at a time."

"I hope so," Tory replied. "I've never seen a real ghost before."

"I told you, it's just swamp gas," Erin insisted.

"Whatever you say," Tory said with a mischievous grin. She had finally found something interesting to do with her vacation.

🐾 🐾 🐾

It was a lovely spring afternoon. The sky was perfectly clear, and a mild wind blowing from the south had nudged the temperature all the way up to 60 degrees.

Here, deep in the Michigan woods, Old Man Winter's retreat was celebrated by the mating calls of jays and robins, the raspy grunts of toads, and the crackling of leaves as rabbits scampered through the undergrowth in search of new burrows.

These sounds were joined by the footsteps and voices of two young teenage girls as they made their way through the reawakening forest.

"Come on, Erin, don't be such a wuss," Tory called. "Let's pick up the pace!"

"I'm tired," Erin moaned as she struggled to keep up with her energetic cousin. "We've been out here for an hour. How 'bout we turn back and go home?"

"But I'm just getting warmed up," Tory said, doing a series of deep knee bends to keep herself limber and maintain her elevated heart rate. "Fifteen more minutes, then we'll turn back."

Tory stood upright and sucked in a deep breath. She loved the smell of the clean, moist air here in the woods, and enjoyed the feel of cool earth cushioned by a bed of leaves beneath her feet. It reminded her of the hilly forests of her native Eugene, only here the trees were mostly a leafy variety rather than the firs and pines she was used to back in Oregon. She gazed up at the stark, skeletal limbs around her and imagined them bursting with greenery just a few weeks from now. She was disappointed she would not be around to see the show. The landscape would be even more spectacular come September when these woods would be ablaze with the fiery reds, oranges, golds, and yellows of autumn. In Oregon, Tory thought, they basically had two seasons—warm-and-dry and cold-and-wet, with few of the landscape changes that accompanied the flow of seasons here in the Midwest.

Tory wanted to experience this environment as much as she could before returning home in three days, and was frustrated by her cousin Erin's lack of enthusiasm, not to mention endurance.

"Forget it, Tory," Erin said, still gasping for breath. "If you want to keep stumbling around in the mud, be my guest. Me, I'm going to go home and watch TV or something."

"Knock yourself out," Tory said sarcastically. "I'll be back by dinnertime."

"You sure you can find your way back?" Erin asked, scanning the surrounding forest.

"No problem," Tory assured her. "There's a compass inside my head. I never get lost."

"Then have fun," Erin said, turning around. "I'll see you back at the house."

With that, Erin began stumbling down the path in the direction from which they'd come.

Tory didn't waste a second before continuing on her way. She knew that the best way to enjoy a hike was to keep moving, since resting only encouraged the muscles to relax, which then required you to exert twice as much effort to get them back up to speed. Besides, Tory never liked to stand still.

About 10 minutes after she and her cousin had parted company, Tory found herself approaching a small, muddy stream. The water, which was virtually covered with dead leaves, made a faint gurgling sound as it slowly snaked its way through the forest.

"No problem," Tory said to herself. She took a few steps back, then broke into a run and gracefully leaped across the tiny brook. She landed with a *plop* on the far side. At the same moment there was a bright flash of light, and for a second Tory was blinded and disoriented.

She shook her head and her vision immediately returned.

"Wow," she said aloud. "What was that about?"

Tory suddenly felt tingles rush down her spine. She had the strangest feeling that there was someone else in the woods with her. Her heart beating wildly, she spun around and was shocked to find herself gazing into an eerie yellow-orange light.

The light appeared to be about the size of a basketball and hovered at eye level above the muddy ground. Its glow was just bright enough to be seen in the shadowy daylight, but dull enough so that Tory could see through it to the forest beyond.

"Will-o'-the-Wisp," Tory said aloud, immediately recognizing the phenomenon.

Tory recalled her cousin Erin's boring "scientific"

explanation, but when she sniffed the air, she could detect no trace of methane. If this strange light was truly caused by swamp gas, it was oddly odorless.

As Tory watched in amazement, the ball of yellow-orange light suddenly shot across to her left, zigzagged between several oak trees, and then, in a flash, appeared directly behind her.

Tory spun around quickly, nearly slipping on the slick, muddy ground.

The ghostly light hovered just three feet in front of her, its body pulsing with a warm, inviting glow. The feeling Tory had experienced when she first saw this "thing" from her cousin's window returned. She seemed to sense *intelligence* radiating from it, and had the unmistakable feeling that this seemingly formless ball of light was *alive*.

The light continued to hang suspended in front of her, as if it were studying her. Tory's curiosity totally overwhelmed any sense of fear, and she slowly reached out her right hand to touch it.

With aching slowness, her fingers approached the pulsing orb. As they did, she could feel warmth radiating from it. It was a pleasant, comforting sensation, one that reminded her of sitting around a glowing fireplace on a cold winter's night.

Tory's index finger was just about to touch the outer edge of the orb when it quickly darted away. Tory spun about, trying to locate it, and for a moment feared she'd lost it forever.

But then something compelled her to turn to her left, and when she did, she saw the ball of light floating just in front of a stand of birch trees.

"There you are," she found herself saying. "You can hear me, can't you?"

As if in response, the orb glowed brightly for the briefest of moments, then returned to its dull yellow-orange color.

"You're not swamp gas," Tory said, suddenly sure of herself. "Is it true what my cousin Erin said? Are you a ghost?"

The light appeared to hesitate this time, then it ducked behind the thick trunk of a large oak tree. After a few seconds it emerged halfway out of its hiding place. It was as if it were *peeking* out at Tory, teasing her.

"Don't be shy," Tory said, extending an open hand. "I'm not going to hurt you. I'd like to be your friend."

Now the light emerged fully and flashed brightly once more. Moving faster than the eye could follow, it zoomed over to Tory and flitted playfully over her head.

Tory laughed almost uncontrollably as she gazed up in delight at the incredible display above her. She could not take her eyes off the light. She was convinced that this ball of energy *was* alive. More than that, it had a childlike personality, and it wanted to play.

Giggling like a schoolgirl, Tory reached up and touched the outer edge of the light, feeling a warm glow pass through her as she did.

"Tag, you're it!" she cried, tearing off into the trees.

The light hesitated only a second before zooming after her. As Tory stumbled through the thick, shadowy woods, the light flitted in and out among the nearby trees, circling teasingly before finally dive-bombing her from directly overhead.

Tory fell to the earth and clutched her side laughing

hysterically. She couldn't remember ever feeling this free and giddy. There was something about this ghostly light that conjured up all the childlike feelings and emotions she'd been struggling to bury as she entered young adulthood. The sensation was truly liberating, and she wished it could last forever.

Having "tagged" Tory, the light now retreated several yards and waited for her to recover. Caked with mud and dead leaves, Tory stumbled to her feet and pretended to glare at the taunting orb.

"I'm gonna get you!" she announced, then broke into a run. The ghostly light flitted in and out among the tree trunks, always letting Tory get within striking distance before suddenly pulling away.

The chase continued like this for several more minutes until, still pursuing the light, Tory stumbled into what she thought was a shallow mud puddle. But as she tried to extricate herself, she found her legs sinking deeper and deeper into the soft, liquid earth.

"Hey, what's going on?" she cried as she continued to struggle. The mud seemed to have an unnatural grip on her, and the more she tried to free her legs, the deeper she seemed to sink.

And then she remembered what her cousin Erin had said. *Quicksand!* It was quicksand that had supposedly killed that girl 50 years earlier. And now this very same quicksand was threatening to kill her, too!

"Help!" Tory cried at the top of her lungs. "Somebody help me!"

She could hear her cries echoing through the trees, but all she heard in return was the rustling of the wind and the songs of distant birds. She was alone in these woods. There was no one to come help her, no one to free her from death's insistent grasp.

With pleading eyes, she looked up at the glowing light that now hovered just out of her reach.

"You did this, didn't you?" she whispered. "You lured me here. Why? Why do you want me to die?"

The light just continued to hang in the air. And then it vanished, as did Tory Brand beneath the muddy surface.

ᚠ ᚠ ᚠ

"There are those two lights again," Joyce Connors said, pointing out the family's living room window. "There, out in the trees."

"I see them," her younger sister, Diane, replied. "Is it true they're ghosts?"

"Some folks call 'em 'Will-o'-the-Wisp,'" their grandmother said, joining the girls at the window. "The scientists say they're just swamp gas. But the folks around here, well, some say they are ghosts—ghosts of girls who got lost in the woods a long, long time ago."

"What do you think they are, Grandma Erin?" Joyce said, looking into her grandmother's long oval face.

"Just swamp gas, sweetheart," Erin said with a sigh. "But stay out of those woods just the same."

"Tomorrow, we'll go take a look for ourselves," Joyce whispered to her sister.

"Good idea," Diane agreed. "I've never seen a real ghost."

THE SKEPTIC

❧

"**S**O, HOW DO YOU LIKE LIVING IN A HAUNTED house?" Johnny Gleason asked Carter Mobley as they waited for their seventh-period math class to begin.

"What are you talking about?" Carter replied, looking up from the homework he was supposed to turn in that day. His blond crew cut glistened under the room's fluorescent lighting, and his T-shirt, which bore the logo of a famous athletic shoe manufacturer, displayed several fresh red stains from the spaghetti lunch he'd enjoyed earlier that afternoon.

"You live in that old stucco house down at the end of La Paz Court, don't you?" Johnny inquired. "The one with the orange tile roof?"

"Yeah," Carter replied, picturing the classical Spanish-style two-story home his family recently bought when his father was transferred to Los Angeles from Bakersfield, over 100 miles to the north.

"Well, didn't anyone tell you?" Johnny continued, his voice lowering to a whisper. "That house is full of ghosts."

"No way," Carter scoffed.

"It's true," Johnny whispered, leaning in toward Carter conspiratorially. He brushed his long brown hair away from his eyes and flashed a wicked smile that clearly displayed his silver braces. "I knew a kid who lived there back in second grade. His name was Alan Brooks. He used to talk about weird stuff going on in that house all the time. He'd hear things banging in the middle of the night. Moans coming from inside the walls. Once he even saw the ghost of an old man coming up the stairs."

"And he told you all this in second grade," Carter said skeptically, remembering some of the tall tales *he* told when he was that age. Once, when he was eight, he'd told his friends that his dad worked for the CIA. Later that same year he'd insisted that his name was really Oogla Klexpan, and that he was a visitor from the planet Zinnya in the Alpha Centauri star system. That particular charade had gone on for two entire months and was embellished with such imaginative detail that he'd practically convinced himself he was an alien. Compared to that, Alan Brooks's stories about things going bump in the night seemed like Amateur Hour.

"Hey, I know it sounds crazy, but things got so bad there that the Brookses finally had to leave," Johnny stated. "Since then, I don't think a family's been able to stay in that house for more than a year or so before moving out. Didn't the real estate agent who sold you the place tell you all this? I think it's in the law that they have to."

"Actually, my dad's company found the house for us," Carter explained. "We didn't use an agent." "Too bad," Johnny said, sliding into his chair just as their teacher, Mrs. Hirsch, entered the buzzing classroom. "I guess now you're stuck with the place. And the ghosts."

"I don't believe in ghosts," Carter said as he, too, settled into his plastic-backed chair. "Just like I don't believe in flying saucers, ESP, reincarnation, Bigfoot, the Loch Ness Monster, horoscopes, or spontaneous human combustion."

"Then what *do* you believe in?" Johnny asked.

Carter didn't even hesitate before he replied, "Science."

⚡ ⚡ ⚡

Although Carter's father had never worked for the CIA, he *was* an electronics engineer who did, in fact, often do jobs for the U.S. government. Carter had learned a lot from his father, especially about how to judge things with a critical eye.

"Remember, when it comes to the unexplained, the simplest solutions are usually the right ones," his dad was fond of saying. Some of his other favorite expressions included, "Extraordinary claims require equally extraordinary evidence" and "When you hear hoofbeats, think horses before you think zebras."

It was through his father that Carter learned to control his imagination, to look at events with a clear, critical eye. He learned to be skeptical about unusual things that people claimed to have seen or heard, since human senses and human memory are notoriously unreliable. He was taught to demand proof for outrageous claims—the kind of proof that could withstand close scrutiny—and to differentiate between hard facts and mere wishful thinking.

Some people found Carter's skepticism off-putting. Especially kids. Back in Bakersfield his friends seemed to really enjoy talking about UFOs and New Age mysticism, but Carter could never get in on the fun. Despite the practical jokes he once tried to pull off about aliens and the CIA, he knew that, in the adult world, it was tough, hard-nosed thinking that made people successful. People like his dad.

That night, when Carter returned home, he took a few moments to look around his house. Although the house was reportedly built sometime in the late 1920s, it had been remodeled and renovated numerous times over the years, so its interior appeared as fresh and modern as any of the brand-new tract houses that were being built in the city's surrounding suburbs. The decorating, which had been supervised by his mother, a professional interior designer, was Danish modern, featuring lots of leather and exposed wood. The living room had a beautifully polished hardwood floor and was filled with green plants. They had installed lots of track lighting to compensate for the small number of windows — an architectural necessity in Southern California in the years before the invention of air conditioning. Overall, the house was warm and inviting— not the kind of place you'd expect to be plagued by ghosts. Carter almost laughed out loud when he thought about his friend Johnny's claim of ghostly hauntings. The whole idea was downright ridiculous.

But that night, after Carter had gone to bed, he began to entertain the notion that perhaps this place did, indeed, house more than just Carter's family. Lying under his covers, gazing up at the dark plaster ceiling bathed in indistinct shadows, he had the strange feeling that there was another presence in the room with him. It wasn't anything he could see or hear or smell. It was just a feeling deep in the pit of his stomach that someone was watching him.

"Stop it," he scolded himself out loud. "You're letting your imagination get the best of you. You know darned well there's no such thing as ghosts!"

He turned over on his side, buried his head in his pillow, and tried to relax.

Then he heard the sound. Just outside his bedroom, a floorboard creaked. Carter's eyes immediately snapped open and he bolted upright in bed. His ears pricked up as he focused his attention on his door, waiting for another sound.

But he could only hear the muted hum of distant motor traffic . . . and the rapid gasps that were his own breathing.

Then he heard it again. It was the groan and snap of a floorboard, the sound of someone stepping on a piece of loose wood. But who would be moving outside his room at eleven-thirty at night? His parents had gone to bed the same time he had. They had no reason to be roaming the halls at this hour. And besides, if his parents *were* up, they'd be making more noise. They wouldn't be taking one tentative step every five minutes.

If there's a ghost out there, I'm going to see it for myself, he thought. Mustering his courage, he slowly slid himself out of bed, stood up, and crept over to his door. He stopped and listened closely. He heard only chilling silence. And then—*pop!* Another floorboard creaked.

Without stopping to think, Carter grabbed the knob and flung open his bedroom door. There, in the hallway, he saw . . . absolutely nothing. There were no transparent apparitions. No floating specters. Not even a set of glowing red eyes.

Pop! This time the sound came from one of the nearby

walls. Carter still wasn't sure what was making this disturbing noise, but he was certain it wasn't a ghost.

𖧥 𖧥 𖧥

"The house is settling," his father explained over breakfast the next morning. "Parts of it shift as it settles into the earth, which causes the wood to make noises as it's strained and stretched."

"But this house is over 70 years old!" Carter exclaimed. "Can it still be settling after all these years?"

"Some houses *never* settle completely," his mother stated. "The ground is shifting all the time. The water table rises and falls. And remember, here in Southern California, literally dozens of minor earthquakes happen every day. Any one of these things can cause a house like this to make noise."

"Does this make sense to you?" Carter's dad asked.

"Perfect sense," Carter noted. He was glad to have a rational explanation for the things he'd heard the night before. His belief in science demanded one. Now he could sleep peacefully with the knowledge that, despite what his friend Johnny had said, his new house was definitely *not* haunted.

But three nights later, his faith in the rational was once more put to the test. At three o'clock in the morning he was awakened by a low moaning sound, like someone was in terrible pain. Initially, Carter tried to dismiss the sound as something left over from a dream, but when he tried to fall back to sleep, the awful sound returned.

Once again he could feel his heart pounding in his chest, and his breathing became labored as adrenaline pumped through his veins. His muscles tightened and he began to shiver uncontrollably.

"This is ridiculous," Carter whispered to himself. "There's no such thing as ghosts."

Determined to find the rational explanation for this unearthly sound, Carter once again slid out of bed and opened his door. The sound was even more distinct now, a deep, soulful moaning like the plaintive cries of a lost soul.

Moving quietly, his senses on full alert, Carter crept down the carpeted stairs to the ground floor. When he reached the living room, it sounded as if an agonized spirit was right there in the room with him.

Carter turned from side to side, trying to isolate the source of the disturbing noise. It seemed to get louder as he approached the window behind one of the leather-backed reading chairs.

Then he felt a warm breeze pass over him, like an invisible spirit had just brushed past his face. But this was no poltergeist he had just encountered, Carter realized. It was a gust of wind blowing in through a window that someone in the family had failed to close properly. The fabled Santa Ana winds were blowing tonight, bringing gusts of hot air in off the deserts to the north. As they passed through the crack between the window pane and the sill, they made a low moaning sound, not unlike a distant train whistle.

Relieved that he'd once again established a rational explanation for the "ghostly" goings-on in the house, Carter grabbed hold of the wooden window frame and heaved it shut. The moaning sounds immediately ceased.

"I ain't 'fraid of no ghosts," Carter said to himself, quoting a popular movie about the supernatural from the 1980s.

Ready to go back to sleep, Carter moved cautiously up the darkened stairs and found his way to his bedroom. He climbed back into his still-warm bed, pulled the sheets up over himself, and fluffed up his pillow, hoping that sleep would quickly return.

But just as he was dozing off, he was jolted awake by a tremendous *bang!* Thrown from his bed by a powerful force, he found himself lying facedown on the floor, his face buried in his deep pile carpet.

"What the . . . ?" he groaned as he tried to sit up, only to drop back to the floor from dizziness. All kinds of possible scenarios began running through his mind. Could a bomb have gone off near the house? Maybe there had been an earthquake. Or maybe—just maybe—a vengeful spirit had attacked him in his bed.

"There's no such thing as ghosts!" he reminded himself, then struggled to his feet. He stopped short and nearly screamed aloud when he suddenly found himself looking at another boy!

The intruder, who was lying asleep in his bed, appeared to be eight or nine years old, with mid-length brown hair. At first Carter thought this might be a ghost—perhaps the spirit of a boy who'd died here years earlier—but he appeared to be perfectly solid. Not only that, he was wearing pajamas featuring characters from a popular kids' show that had premiered that very year.

"Hey, wake up!" Carter demanded. "Who are you and what are you doing in my bed?"

The strange boy sighed, then turned over on the pillow. Increasingly angry, Carter reached down and shook the intruder by the shoulder.

"Hey, you, wake up!" Carter commanded. Groggy, the boy turned back toward Carter and weakly opened his eyes. A moment passed, then the younger boy bolted up in bed, his eyes suddenly as big as dinner plates.

"Ahhhhhh!" he screamed.

The boy hadn't even finished his horrified wail before Carter was out of the door and racing down the hall to his parents' bedroom. He banged open their door and raced to the foot of their queen-size bed.

"Mom! Dad! Wake up!" he cried. "There's some strange kid in my bed! You've got to do something!"

"Mom! Dad! Wake up!" he heard someone shouting behind him. Spinning around, he was stunned to see the younger, pajama-clad boy stumbling through the door.

There was motion from the bed, a light snapped on, and a man and a woman sat up bleary-eyed. But these were not Carter's parents. In fact, he'd never seen either of them before in his life.

"Jimmy, what's wrong?" the mother asked, shaking the sleep from her head.

"I-I-I think I just saw a ghost," the boy stammered back.

"Now, Jimmy, you know what we told you about—" the man began.

"I'm not making this up!" the boy interrupted. "I felt someone shake my shoulder, and when I woke up, he was standing next to me."

"What did he look like?" the mother asked, not even acknowledging Carter's presence in the room. In fact, *none* of these people seemed to notice Carter standing among them.

"He looked like an older kid, maybe 12 or 13," the boy immediately replied. "And it looked like he was wearing pajamas—" He stopped short as an idea hit him. "Hey, you know that kid who was killed here about 10 years ago during the big earthquake?"

"You mean Carter Mobley?" said the boy's father.

A frigid chill tingled Carter's spine. They were talking about him! But what did they mean when they mentioned a "big earthquake" occurring "10 years ago"?

"I think maybe that was him!" Jimmy said, his voice shaking. "I think maybe that was his—his—*ghost!*"

Carter wanted desperately to say something, to tell these people that he was standing right here, that he wasn't really dead. But he was too frightened to say even a word. Had he been killed that night the Santa Ana winds had been blowing? Was his restless spirit doomed to roam this big old house for—how long?

Forever?

He couldn't even bring himself to think about it. After all, he was Carter Mobley. And he didn't believe in ghosts.

DETHMAN

⟫⊷⊶⊷⊖⊷⊶⊷⊶⊶

ACHIN: *Anyone heard about this new "broadband" technology?*
CUB74: *It's some kind of new cable system.*
GLXYMAN: *It's supposed to increase modem speeds by something like 5,000 percent.*
CUB74: *Also connects to your TV. Transmits digitally.*
GLXYMAN: *Way cool.*
ACHIN: *So when are we gonna get it?*
DETHMAN: *My city's being wired right now. They say it will be nationwide in five years.*
CUB74: *Can't wait that long.*
ACHIN: *Me neither.*
GLXYMAN: *I'm with you, ACHIN.*
DETHMAN: *More Power!*

ᛉ ᛉ ᛉ

ALEX CHIN, SCREEN NAME "ACHIN," WAITED UNTIL the "It's Now Safe to Turn off Your Computer" message flashed on his monitor screen, then deftly snapped off the power. Instantly the hum of the central processor's cooling fan, which had been whirring steadily for the past two hours, fell silent.

"You'd better get yourself down here or you're going to miss supper!" Alex's mother called from the kitchen.

"I told you, I'll be down in a minute!" Alex shouted back. "It takes time to shut down the computer!"

A minute later Alex bounded into the kitchen where his mother, father, and 17-year-old sister, Lillia, were already finishing off their salads.

"So, what's for dinner?" he asked, sliding into his chair. "Whatever it is, it smells good."

"It's baked salmon," replied his father, whose turn it was to make dinner that evening. "I hope you'll have time to enjoy it."

Alex knew what was coming next. It was going to be the world-famous "you spend too much time on the computer" speech. His mother would say that he needed to get out more, to play outside with friends. His dad would then insist that he spend more time on his homework, even though he usually managed to finish it while still at school and was having no trouble maintaining a solid A-minus average. Finally his sister would called him a "geek," "nerd," or some such name to express her disapproval over his choice of leisure-time activities.

He wasn't disappointed.

"I really think you're spending too much time on that computer of yours," his mother said, right on cue. "An hour or so a day is fine, but you seem to be on that thing constantly. A growing boy needs fresh air. Exercise. You should spend more time outside."

Alex immediately turned to his father like a director waiting for an actor to speak his next scripted line.

"Why don't you try reading for a change?" his father

asked. "We have a whole library full of books here. Improve your mind instead of wasting your time in those silly chat rooms."

"Oh, don't be so hard on Alex, guys," Lillia insisted. "He can't help it if he's a cybergeek."

"In case none of you has noticed, computers happen to be the fastest growing area of technology in the country," Alex finally replied in his defense. "You want me to meet people, Mom? Every day I talk to more people than you even *see*, and they're from all over the world. Dad, you want me to 'improve my mind'? What's more educational than learning how to operate computers and surf the Net? I have access to more information than in a *hundred* libraries." Finally he turned with confidence to his big sister. "And, for your information, Lillia, it's us 'cybergeeks' who now control the world. If all the computers in America crashed tomorrow, the whole planet would be plunged right back into the Dark Ages. So *there!*"

Alex looked at his family, who sat in stunned silence. Obviously, they hadn't been expecting such an impassioned, well-considered response from him. He couldn't help but feel a tinge of triumph.

"Well, I still think you need more fresh air," his mother finally said, finishing off her salad.

"And you need to study more," said his father, heading over to the oven.

"Loser," his sister scoffed.

Alex just let out a weary sigh.

帑 帑 帑

ACHIN: *My parents are jerks. My sister is worse. They just don't understand computers.*

DETHMAN: *I hear you, ACHIN. My dad still thinks a RAM is some kind of pickup truck. My mom wouldn't know a byte if it bit her.*

ACHIN: *Parents can be such idiots.*

DETHMAN: *Copy that. My folks were always ragging on me about how much time I spent on-line. They said I was wasting my time. That I should be doing something constructive, like reading a book.*

ACHIN: *They sound just like my folks! How did you make them stop?*

DETHMAN: *I didn't. I just don't listen to them anymore.*

ACHIN: *Good for you. Too bad we can't meet face-to-face. It'd be fun to hang out.*

DETHMAN: *Isn't that what we're doing now?*

ACHIN: *Yeah, I guess it is.*

DETHMAN: *We're friends, ACHIN. Nobody else understands you like I do. We have to stick together.*

ACHIN: *I copy that, DETHMAN.*

⚛ ⚛ ⚛

Alex had first encountered the kid who called himself "DETHMAN" while in a computer gaming chat room two weeks earlier. Although he still had no idea what the boy looked like or where he was from, he had managed to pull a few personal details out of him. For example, he knew that DETHMAN was 13 years old and had been heavily into computers for the past eight years. The guy had a state-of-the-art system with a superfast processor and more than twice the random access memory (RAM) of Alex's system.

86

Plus his house had been wired for broadband, which meant he was able to transmit and receive information virtually instantaneously.

Like Alex, DETHMAN spent most of his free time on-line and enjoyed talking with like-minded kids all over the world. The guy, whoever he was, was smart, funny, and very passionate about computers.

It was good to have a friend like DETHMAN . . . even if he was just words on a computer screen.

牀 牀 牀

TO: ACHIN@lifenet.com
FROM: DETHMAN@cyberlink.com
DATE: 4/7
SUBJECT: No Show
Hey, jerkface. You were supposed to be in the CyberDiner chatroom last night at 9 P.M. Where the heck were you? I don't like being stood up. Next time you make an appointment, keep it. Or else. We'll talk tonight. No excuses.

As Alex stared at the E-mail message on his monitor screen, his brow furrowed with concern. He'd felt bad about missing his scheduled on-line meeting with DETHMAN the previous evening, but his sister's high school band had a concert he'd been forced to attend. He'd been planning to apologize to DETHMAN the next time they were in contact, but now it was too late. DETHMAN was clearly upset. Alex hoped he could make amends.

牀 牀 牀

DETHMAN: *Apology accepted—this time. Now how about we head over to the Digital Arcade and play a few hours of Mutant Attack?*

ACHIN: *I'd love to, but my folks have a new rule: I can't be on the computer after nine o'clock. They think I'm becoming obsessed.*

DETHMAN: *Tell your parents to bug off.*

ACHIN: *I can't do that.*

DETHMAN: *What are you? Some kind of wimp?*

ACHIN: *Hey, they paid for this computer.*

DETHMAN: *So? They gave it to you. That makes it your personal property. If they take it away from you, it's theft.*

ACHIN: *You're crazy, you know that?*

DETHMAN: *Don't call me crazy.*

ACHIN: *Sorry.*

DETHMAN: *Nobody calls me crazy. Nobody!*

ACHIN: *Yeah, fine. Look, I gotta go.*

DETHMAN: *We're not through here, ACHIN. We're gonna play Mutant Attack. We're gonna play all night.*

ACHIN: *I don't think so. Bye. :-O*

☩ ☩ ☩

Alex sighed nervously as he clicked himself out of the CyberDiner chat room. That last conversation had really upset him. Something about DETHMAN's tone was downright unnerving. It reminded him of a horror movie he'd seen about a jealous girl who, after being rejected by her boyfriend, proceeded to cut up the guy's family with a butcher knife. True, it wasn't like he and DETHMAN were dating or anything, but still, jealousy could be a very powerful and dangerous thing. He decided to stay away from DETHMAN for the next few days, just to let things cool down.

Instead, he clicked himself over into another Web site he always enjoyed, The Star Fighters Fan Club. It was a site dedicated to the *Star Fighters* movie series, something he was almost as passionate about as computers.

⚡ ⚡ ⚡

ACHIN: So, has anyone heard about when the next SF movie is coming out?

LARRY56: Sometime next summer, I hear.

NICEGIRL: It should be June 4. They always release the Star Fighters movies on June 4. It's their lucky day or something.

ACHIN: I'm gonna be first in line.

LARRY56: You'll have to get in behind me.

DETHMAN: Well, hello, ACHIN. So there you are.

ACHIN: DETHMAN? What are you doing here?

DETHMAN: You didn't think you could get away from me that easy, did you?

LARRY56: Hey, what's going on here?

DETHMAN: I thought we were friends, ACHIN.

ACHIN: Just leave me alone, okay?

DETHMAN: Friends don't dump on friends.

NICEGIRL: Geez, why don't you two get a private chat room or something? We're trying to talk Star Fighters here.

DETHMAN: You're not getting away with this, ACHIN. Wherever you go, I'll find you. You need me.

Alex signed off from his on-line service and quickly shut down his computer. There was now no question about it: DETHMAN was a wacko. A nutcase. Two cans short of a six-pack. Alex was sorry he'd ever started up a conversation with the guy.

At first Alex wondered how DETHMAN had managed to find him at the Star Fighters Web site, but then remembered that they'd talked at length about the popular film series during several of their on-line communications. It didn't take a rocket scientist to figure out he might go to the site after leaving the CyberDiner.

Fortunately there were dozens of similar Star Fighters-related sites on the Web, as well as hundreds of other places he could go if he wanted to talk to other kids without being hounded by DETHMAN. This wasn't like dealing with a real-life flesh-and-blood stalker who knew where you lived and where you went to school, and could follow your every move if he wanted to. No, if nothing else, the Internet offered complete anonymity.

If DETHMAN thought he could intimidate Alex into renewing their friendship, he was going to be disappointed.

⚜ ⚜ ⚜

There were over 50 E-mail messages waiting in Alex's on-line mailbox when he signed on the following afternoon. They were all from DETHMAN. Their tone ranged from apologetic to overtly threatening. Clearly, this DETHMAN kid did *not* like being rejected.

DETHMAN's assaults, even though they were only electronic, were giving Alex the creeps. They made him feel, well, violated, like his privacy was being invaded. He didn't know what to do, so he explained his situation to his mother and father at dinner.

"I think you're right. This DETHMAN kid has a few screws loose," his father agreed.

"That's what happens when you sit in front of the

computer all day and all night," his mother scolded. "Your brains get fried."

"So what am I supposed to do?" Alex pleaded. "I'm afraid to even log on anymore because my entire mailbox is going to be jammed with messages from this guy."

"Well, you can change your code name, can't you?" his father suggested. "With a new name, DETHMAN won't be able to find you."

The solution was so simple, Alex was surprised he hadn't thought of it himself. All he had to do was log on to his on-line service, go into the Customer Service area, hit a few command buttons, and DETHMAN would be out of his life forever. What could be easier?

As soon as dinner was over, Alex raced up to his bedroom, booted up his computer, and logged on to his on-line service. As expected, his E-mail box was filled with yet more messages from DETHMAN. In fact, he'd transmitted so many letters that the mailbox was actually full and unable to accept any more communications.

"Go bother someone else," Alex said to himself as he clicked on the Customer Service icon. Less than two minutes later, he was traveling the Information Superhighway under a brand-new name: FIGHTER-FAN.

His first move after assuming the new moniker was to visit UFO-tainment, a site devoted to flying saucers and other things extraterrestrial.

DETHMAN was waiting for him.
DETHMAN: Hello, ACHIN. Or should I call you Alex?
FIGHTER-FAN: DETHMAN, how did you know it was me?
DETHMAN: I have ways. I told you, Alex, you can't get away

from me that easy. You can change your name all you want, but I'll find you. We need each other.

⁂ ⁂ ⁂

"I'm contacting Cyberlink," said Alex's dad, referring to the popular on-line service through which DETHMAN was communicating. "There are laws against using the Internet to harass people. They'll find this DETHMAN and disconnect him."

"Thanks, Dad," Alex said gratefully. "This guy is really driving me crazy. He's like a stalker. I know it sounds weird, but I've got a feeling he's going to show up at our front door one of these days."

"That's not going to happen, I promise you," his father assured him. "We're going to delete DETHMAN from your life once and for all."

⁂ ⁂ ⁂

It took nearly a week for the representative from Cyberlink to respond to Mr. Chin's complaint. The message arrived in the form of an E-mail message that was nearly as upsetting as DETHMAN's constant stream of threats and apologies.

"Cyberlink says they had a subscriber who called himself DETHMAN, but his account was terminated last year, and no one new is registered with that name," Alex told his parents, showing them a hard copy of the E-mail message.

"Maybe he's using another Internet service," his father proposed.

"I don't think so," Alex said, his voice shaking. "The reason DETHMAN was disconnected was because he died."

⚛ ⚛ ⚛

"Dennis just loved his computer," said the female voice on the phone. "He was on it night and day. He wouldn't watch television or listen to music. He just wanted to be on his computer."

It had taken all the courage Alex could muster to contact Mrs. Nussbaum, who, according to Cyberlink, was the mother of the boy who'd called himself DETHMAN. Although he felt very embarrassed about talking to a mother who'd recently lost her child, he felt he needed to tell her what was happening to him. He wasn't sure why.

"Excuse me for asking this, Mrs. Nussbaum," Alex said hesitantly. "but could you tell me how your son, Dennis, died?"

"Actually, he died while he was on the computer," Mrs. Nussbaum replied.

"How did *that* happen?" Alex asked in disbelief.

"It was during a thunderstorm," the woman explained. "Our house was hit by lightning. Poor Dennis was typing something on the keyboard at the time, and the charge went right through the computer into him. I got to his room just seconds after it happened, but it was already too late. My son was gone."

Just then, the truth hit Alex like the lightning bolt that had struck Dennis Nussbaum. Dennis—or DETHMAN, as he liked to call himself—wasn't quite dead. Not in the conventional sense. The powerful electrical blast that had electrocuted his body had also done something to his mind, releasing it from the confines of mortal tissue and sending it, in the form of billions of bits of data, back through the telephone lines into that web of linked computers called the Internet.

DETHMAN was a cyberghost.

☩ ☩ ☩

"It's so good to see you off that computer," Alex's mother said approvingly as the family gathered in the living room to watch TV. "Now you can spend more time with us."

"Oh, goody," his sister, Lillia, said sarcastically.

"So why the sudden change of interests?" his father inquired as he reached for the remote control.

"Just got tired of the computer, that's all," Alex replied. He didn't dare tell anyone the truth, that he was being stalked by the spirit of a dead cybernerd, and the only way to avoid him was to stay away from his or any other computer.

"Well, I think you'll find *this* interesting," his dad said, clicking on the TV. "I just had the cable company upgrade us to broadband. You know what that is?"

"That's a new kind of cable, isn't it?" Lillia asked.

"It's got a hundred times the capacity of the old coaxial cable we used to have," Alex's dad said proudly. "We can get more channels . . . and digital pictures. And the TV's automatically hooked to the Internet. Not that we'll waste our time with *that* feature. . . . "

"No!" Alex cried, rising to his feet. But it was too late. The picture on the TV screen flickered for a moment, then became filled with the weird, haunted face of a young teenage boy.

"Hello, Alex. I've missed you," the boy said in an odd, mechanical voice.

"Who's *that?*" Lillia asked in shock.

Alex grabbed the remote control from his dad's hand and furiously clicked the channel-change button. But it was useless. The strange, not-quite-human face was on every channel.

"You can't get away from me, Alex," the face on the screen announced. "Wherever you go, I'll be there. Day or night. At home or at school. Wherever there's a computer or a TV, that's where I'll be. We're gonna be buddies for life."

Alex's jaw dropped and his blood ran cold.

It was DETHMAN.